A Little Too Rambunctious

Written and Illustrated by
Richard Voorhees

Other Works by Richard Voorhees

Shooting Genji (novel)

The World's Oldest Professions
(An Unabridged Dictionary of Work)

Proust + Vermeer (film)

Be-Bop-A-Lula (screenplay)

Old Pros (a blog on the history of professions)

A Season of Haikus (poems)

The Roll Call of Ghosts (play)

A Little Too Rambunctious

Written and Illustrated by
Richard Voorhees

FOUND ART PUBLISHING
SAN FRANCISCO, CALIFORNIA

Illustrations by Richard Voorhees.
Book design by JM Shubin, BookAlchemist.net

Publisher's Cataloging-in-Publication data

Voorhees, Richard.
 A Little Too Rambunctious
 Written and illustrated by Richard Voorhees.
 pages cm
 ISBN 9780990626473

1. Childhood–Fiction. 2. Friendship –Fiction.
3. Family–Fiction. 4. School–Fiction. 5. Teacher-student
relationship–Fiction. 6. Vietnam War, 1961-1975–Fiction. 7.
Seattle (Wash.)–History–20th century–Fiction. I. Title.

PS3622.O693 L58 2015
813.6 --dc23-

First Edition

To my lifelong friend, Kurt Lantz,
the funniest kid in town

Contents

SUMMER

Summer 1968

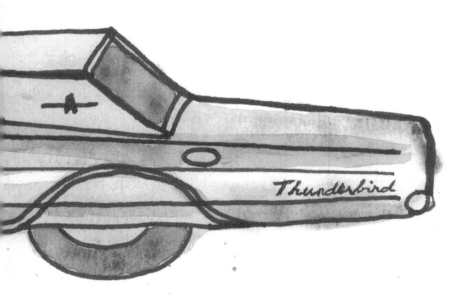

Chapter 1.

It's Right to be Taught by an Enemy

My final report card for fourth grade came in the mail in one of those unmistakable yellow envelopes. I passed, and my grades were even pretty good, but as for my "citizenship," not so much. Apparently I was "a little too rambunctious." (There's a misunderstatement for ya.) Even so, it was no big whoop compared to what came next.

A school administrator had saved the worst for last (and in perfect cursive writing). On the back of my report card was my fifth grade room assignment—I was going to have Miss Salappa, Room 8. I didn't even have time to say "What the...!" *It was already too late.* Terror loped through me like carbonation from a soda taking a slow return trip up my nose.

In immutable red ink the awful news squatted in front of me, toadlike, laying its eggs in my throat, poisoning what should have been a perfectly good summer. My mouth got a metallic bite to it, as if I was sucking a penny.

Why this dread curse on the house of Knowling?

My brother, Yownskins, and my sister, the Onliest,

had already had Salappa. For years I'd heard Salappa horror stories, of her terrorizing her students, constantly getting mad, grinding them down one by one. My heart was being crushed in the icy grip of a weird and grim fate.

It was pretty much impossible to remember how to spell Miss Salappa's name. Get it wrong and you had to put your name on the blackboard and miss gym or recess or lunch or all three. Maybe even stay after school. Was it Miss Sallapa, Sallappa, or Salopa? And just how much was she missing? In Old Finnish, "lapa" means "to lope" or "to leap," which is where we get "to elope." How to avoid becoming an old Lapp, an old maid.

She was Sulla pah pah pah to Wags. And Sullappa to Coolos. She was So Lawppa to Yownskins—spoken with derision, accenting the Lawp. She signed her name Edieberthe Salappa in the yearbook, disguising her madness in perfectly regular cursive writing. It wasn't only anger, was it? In another lifetime, she could have written a hefty instruction manual for the Finnish Inquisition.

According to her permanent record, Salappa was born in 1907 in Embarrass, Minnesota. The coldest spot in the forty-eight states! The strangely named Embarrass is a small town sixty miles from Duluth that was settled by Finnish immigrants in 1895. Sallapa brought a frozen block of Embarrassment with her when she came to Seattle. It seems like she kept it in that icebox where her heart should have been. If she had a heart, it must have been as hard as one of those

Cornish game hens that had been in our freezer since the beginning of the Ice Age.

Summer vacation was evaporating, time accelerating. June was a damp and distant memory. July had charged by. It was the first week in August—the summer was hot for a change, the air thick as jello, the grass totally scorched, just dust and porkypine quills. That afternoon, I was scuffing my way home across the View Ridge Playfield, and I happened to look at the retaining wall on the north side of the park and saw that someone had written "fuc" on it in big black letters. I had to agree. There was nothing to do really but await the arrival of September. The jig was up.

August was like a ferryboat, drifting slowly and rushing headlong, engines conked out, about to jackknife over Snoqualmie Falls and somehow smash into the View Ridge School cafeteria. An auditorium where they dish out meat blanquette with ice cream scoopers. Huge dollops of mashed potatoes swaddled in a meat blanket. August is the Sunday of months. Boring and dread-filled. You can't get it out of your mind that the next day is Monday or the next month is September, bringing with it the first day of the interminable school year, the first Wednesday after Labor Day.

"And I get to get. I hafta get. I gotta get Miss Salappa." They'd reached into the bin of ping-pong balls and my birthday had come up. I objected conscientiously, like mad, but what good did it do me?

When I think about it, landing in Salappa's class may have been a simple case of malice aforethought.

15

Salappa had plucked me from the litter. Having "taught" my siblings, she must have figgered she'd already laid the groundwork to deal with me.

The Roman poet Ovid wrote: "It is right to be taught by an enemy." You might agree. They teach you cause and effect, the pain in a misstep, ambush and punishment, paranoia and stealth, a fine-tuned concentration. In short, a love of learning.

Some scholars, and especially critics, benefit from this kind of punitive learning environment. When they grow up, they never stop reading, straining their eyes over the tiniest print in the dictionary, searching infinite card catalogues, seeking out the rarest archives. Ultimately, what are they after? Revenge. They want to prove somebody wrong. They want to prove 'em wrong.

At the time, all I could think was: What about Mr. Cool? Who'd Coolos get?

Chapter 2.

Mr. Cool

Mr. Cool was my best friend, a kid who refused to be a slave, who was always slipping off his chains. He was a giddy, madcap anarchist on the lam. A sneaky scurrying skidaddling kid sucking in deep gulps of childhood. Running for dear life.

He and I were both the youngest in our families. We both had three older brothers lording it over us. Which taught us the virtue of our spying-then-dashing demeanor.

"Who'd you get?"

"Sullappa!"

"Oh, man, so'd I!"

"Vis, we're fucced." (My real name may be Van Knowling, but Coolos started playing around with my last name, changing it to Vlahas, and then in a moment of inspiration, he boiled it down to Vis.)

"You're tellin' me. My brother and my sister both

had her. She's a complete bitch."

When I found out Mr. Cool was going to be in Sullappa's class too, I figgered maybe it wouldn't be so bad.

"You know if anybody else's got her?"

"You're the first one I called."

"At least we both got her."

"I couldn't take it if I had her all by myself."

"Me neither."

"Coolos, whatya doin' this afternoon?"

"Packin'. We're gonna go away for two weeks to Oregon, to our cabin."

"You are?"

"Yeah. I asked my Dad if I could invite you."

"Yeah?"

"He's gonna be driving down for the weekend. He said you could ride down with him."

"All right! Lemme ask if it's okay, okay?"

"We can play Skeeball in Seaside."

"What's that?"

"You'll see."

"Can we sleep out?"

"Sure. It'll give us time to figger out a plan for Sullappa."

"We'll figger out something."

"Peanut Butter Man!"

"Gotta go, Peanutbuttuhmahn. Gotta grab my broiled bologna sandwich before it burns to a crisp. I'll let ya know if I can come."

Chapter 3.

A Ride in a T-Bird

My parents apparently thought it was a great idea to have me under someone else's feet, so Friday afternoon, Mr. Cool's dad picked me up in his new, white 1968 Thunderbird. Our family had a robin's egg blue 1961 Chevy Impala station wagon. My dad, the Ethical Man, liked cars that were morally incapable of exceeding 65 mph. He had his own idea about the true meaning of practical—the practical family car. Not so, Mr. Cool's dad.

"Is it a long drive to your place in Oregon?"

"Not too long."

Enough chitchat. I don't think we exchanged another word. We hit the open road, and he began to put the accelerator to good use. He didn't say anything like "better buckle up" or "hold onto your hat." He just kept pushing the pedal to the metal and the road roared by, and I squeezed deeper and deeper into my white bucket seat. The yellow hash marks were disappearing under that Thunderbird like tracer bullets. I can only guess what he was thinking: "Only have two days, only two days." Or, "I own a T-Bird, I'm damn well gonna use it." Or maybe, "Let's give this Knowling something to remember me by."

I was playing my greatest game of statue-maker ever. Don't do anything to startle Mr. T-Bird, or strain the shocks, send us careering off the road. Look on the sunny side: this way we'll get to the cabin before sundown, or we'll die, in which case, no fifth grade with Salopa.

This was new. My dad was not in the habit of taking risks while driving and it was one subject he thought important enough to spell out. Usually, I think he thought that leading by example was to be preferred. "The real danger," he would say, "driving on the freeway comes when you have to change lanes. What I find works is to figure out which lane I need to be in to get where I'm going and then to get in that lane and stay there."

He credited William James for his own belief in the virtue of habit. "You don't have to waste your time and energy thinking about small things. You can think about other things than the vagaries of rush-hour traffic." If he'd had his druthers, he wouldn't have driven at all. He liked to read *The Great Books of the Western World* on the bus. He read all of Shakespeare, twice, taking the #7.

My dad did like to scare my mom, though, by making a big show of admiring the scenery while driving in the

Cascades, on mountain roads that had narrow shoulders and sheer cliffs. And if he was really in a good mood, he'd let go of the steering wheel and drive with his knees, and say: "Children, isn't that magnificent?!" and point at the deep green chasms in the distance. Then he would turn to his wife: "Dear, admit it, it's a gorgeous view." She would fight back indirectly: "Your father only does this because he knows it frightens me." But she would eventually break down: "Dear! Please! Stop it!" And we would laugh nervously, Dad getting the better of Mom. Poor dear.

Mr. Cool's dad had a different attitude altogether. Seeing that he didn't believe in routine, I hoped that at least he adhered to the school of calculated risk. Struggling to move, as if I were frozen in a nightmare, slowly, against my quaking will, I leaned over toward the middle-aged businessman and stretched slightly to see the speedometer. We were going 96 miles an hour. I was morbidly impressed. My dad never cracked the speed limit, in fact, he was probably the only person in the entire country who thought it was great when the speed limit was lowered from 70 mph to 55 mph in the 1980s. ("Think of all the lives it will save.") Think of all the vacation eaten up crawling down the highway.

I eased back into my position of absolute balance and thought about how at this clip we would get to their cabin soon and I would get to see Coolos and we'd have a whole weekend to fool around. I performed interstate meditation, a passive yearning to arrive in onepieceness.

Chapter 4.

A Mishap at Sea

My dad drove with his knees mainly when he was leaving for work, creeping down the alley while he put his seat belt on. He didn't want to waste any time, so this was how he buckled up—on the run. Mr. T-Bird wasn't wearing a seat belt. As with so many things, I wasn't sure whether that was a good sign or a bad one. He finally eased off the gas, turned off the highway onto a road overgrown with weeds, and bumped down next to a marshy lake and a white house.

It had been a very lazy afternoon, the kind that businessmen dream of when they drive a hundred miles an hour away from the pressure and drudgery of the city.

That evening, the only sound to be heard was the low farting of an outboard motor propelling a dinghy across a pond. Coolos, his dad, his grandfather, and I were tooling around the little lake next to their place. His brothers and his mom stayed behind. If you own a T-bird, you sure as hell aren't going to row a boat on the weekend, and that outboard was kicking up a breeze that felt nice.

We'd been skimming along for no more than five or ten minutes, when Coolos leaned over the side of their craft and yelped, pointing: "I see a fish!!" "Where?!" I shouted back, looking down the length of his forefinger. ("Just think, a live fish in a real lake. Performing!" This was all pretty new to me.)

As his dad and grandfather turned to look, they all saw my friend's glasses slip off his nose and drop kaplink in the lake and sink. We all watched as they swam out of sight.

His father exploded: "Goddammit!" and slapped his son hard on the side of the head. "Why do you always have to be so stupid?!" Coolos turned bright red and his eyes too, but he didn't cry; though that was the closest I ever saw him come to crying. I wished we could have swum for it. Not for the glasses, for what was left of summer vacation.

"We're going back because of you. Wait 'til your mother hears what a smart kid she's got." Even in the quiet evening, even biting his tongue, you could hear his dad swearing a blue streak in the sputtering of the quarter-horsepower outboard. When his son wasn't looking, the grandfather patted his grandson on the knee. All this anger over a pair of glasses scotch-taped in three places. I was beginning to take a dim view of his dad. He didn't know how to behave on vacation. Lucretius wasn't the last to point out the absurdity of trying to get away on vacation: you always take yourself along.

My dad didn't know how to comport himself on vacation either, but in a different way. Since he wouldn't consider speeding, we always had "a long drive ahead of us." The only solution was to start bright and early. Rousting the troops. Up and adam! At six fifty-five, we were driven from some motel bed out into the parking lot's blinding sun to crawl into the back seats of the '61 Impala.

My mom rode shotgun, tending to the bologna sandwiches, peanut butter, cheese and crackers, milk, ginger snaps, vanilla wafers, and a bushel of apples that she hulled, quartered and passed back to the children. We rolled miles shelling apple seeds with our teeth, the brown hull parting around the white kernal, it in turn parting around the fog of being—the idea of the germ of the root of the apple tree.

Many times over the years, the car door that hadn't been slammed shut flew open and suddenly our mom was pinnioning children in the seat as she gathered the door back in, or calling lifesaving instructions to my brothers to make sure our sister or I didn't get sucked out the open door (like Goldfinger at 30,000 feet).

And in the emergency of somebody about to explode because they had to take a pee so bad, in the middle of a crowded, streaming freeway, miles from an exit ramp—she would pass back an empty milk carton and silently pray we could shoot straight in broad daylight at 65 mph.

Sometimes one of us would notice that the car door wasn't shut and she'd make sure everyone was leaning the other direction before letting "one of the boys open it and give it a good slam this time." Staring out the yawning door, the wind cranked up like a jet engine, the pavement rushing by a blurry foot below, I used to think I could walk away from the roll if I leapt from the moving car.

But not always. More often I imagined what it would be like to race the Impala on foot. I could see myself alongside, keeping up, legs and arms pumping.

My friend's mom was surprised to have us vacationing boaters back so soon. "This stupid kid of yours lost his glasses. He let 'em fall in the middle of the lake." "You what?!" "It was an accident," he murmured keeping his eyes down. "Sometimes I can't believe you, you little idiot. You're hopeless. You're going to pay for those glasses yourself, do you hear me?" "Did you hear what your mother said?" "Yes sir." Aware of me as an unwilling witness, they postponed their rage. "This isn't the end of this, young man." "Yessir."

Later, when we were lying in our cabin bunk-beds, I said kinda lamely, "Maybe we'll find your glasses tomorrow when it's light."

"Yeah, in the middle of the lake."

"What're your parents gonna do?"

"I dunno."

"It's not like you did it on purpose."

"I hope we still get to go to Seaside."

"Me, too."

"Oh, c'mon! Let's get back to 'The Main Subject.'"

"Yeah. 'The Main Subject.'"

"So? Well? Who do you like?"

"Ruthie. Who do you like?"

"You know who... Blarney."

"Blarney. Yeah, but why?"

"She's got a great arm. Nice to have on your team in 'soak 'em.' She can really peg 'em. Why Ruthie?"

"One day, we had to pass our Social Studies tests back, for the person behind us to correct, and the teacher asked Ruthie what I'd put for number five. Ruthie made up an answer for me without waiting a second, pretended I'd gotten it right. I think I left it blank. That was so cool."

Chapter 5.

Skeeball and the Free Ticket

I'd been to Seaside, Oregon before with my family, but I'd never before known the thrilling, musty world of the Skeeball parlor. Mr. Cool's spirits were buoyed by his enthusiasm for Skeeball. The previous night's trauma was forgotten. His parents dropped us off and promised to get us in a couple of hours.

He led the way inside the little shop, the Skeeball parlor. A chubby woman, Madame Skeeball, with limp gray hair combed back in a bun, was standing alone inside, overseeing the potential fun afforded by four wooden Skeeball lanes. The sun drove through the store windows and lit the dust in the air.

"How much is a game?"

"Five cents," she said.

"Then," Coolos told her, "we need a bunch of nickels."

"How many?"

"A bunch. A buck's worth."

"Me, too."

On my usual penny gumball allowance, that was something—to spend a dollar all at once like that.

The woman clicked forty nickels out of her change dispenser.

I waited to follow my friend's lead. He dropped a nickel in the Skeeball machine's maw, pulled a lever, and there and then began the quiet rumble of a distant rockslide. A column of wooden balls rolled into an open slot and clacked to a halt. They were the size of small wooden grapefruit. He took one and rolled it up the lane. It leapt up a ramp at the end of a ten-foot bowling lane and hopped into one of the target's rings, one in a series of concentric circles.

The closer to the center you managed to send your ball, the more points you scored.

Mr. Cool looked over at me and smiled. "Skeeball," is all he said. Then he picked up another wooden ball and hucked it up the lane.

Skeeball, it turned out, is like bowling writ small, perfect for ten-year olds. The room was much smaller than a cavernous bowling alley. The air was filled with the deep reverberation of the wooden Skeeballs rolling and plunging, and the dull clicking stack of their return to the open slot. While some players were bowling, others were waiting for a fresh set of balls to roll back down the chute.

All afternoon, we played Skeeball. If you scored high enough in a game of ten tosses, the woman would give you a yellow ticket (or a couple), off an enormous roll of chit, which could be redeemed for prizes when you called it quits. We were practically gambling!

After you've played any game long enough, you may decide to vary your delivery just for the heck of

knowing you can do it, that you can make a shot six different ways. This isn't the case if your goal is to become a sports juggernaut, "the thing that could not miss." In that case, you stick to the program, practice the same motion again and again and again.

That wasn't for us. Coolos and I threw straight shots, bank shots off the left side board, bank shots off the right side board, spin shots, backspins, hard slamming leapers, finessing tiny lippers. And if the old woman hadn't been there, we'd have probably rolled three balls or five balls at once. We might even have whipped a couple fastballs overhand, caught up in the moment, getting maybe just a little too rambunctious.

When we'd exhausted our supply of nickels, hours later, I had thirty-six yellow tickets and Mr. Cool had thirty-nine. We looked over the shelves of prizes. Plastic pearl necklaces and other useless junk fell within our reach. But there were animals welded out of nuts and bolts that could be had for forty tickets. Mr. Cool gave me the difference so I could get a cool black cat of nuts and bolts.

I'd been shown the lanes by Mr. Cool, the mad Duke of Skeeball, and we'd become masters of chaos.

We played Skeeball one other time. At the amusement park in downtown Seattle (the "Fun Forest") under a cruddy corrugated plastic roof. It was a typical summer day in Seattle—cold, wet, overcast. It wasn't like Seaside, where we'd enjoyed the privacy of our own Skeeball parlor.

Someday, I vowed, I'm gonna have a huge wreck

room with a Skeeball wing. Just a couple Skeeball lanes, fine cigars, cognac, club sandwiches, and a butler to dispense nickels and yellow coupons redeemable. And a snooker table.

Weirdly enough, the Fun Forest had the same tickets. Are these imbued with universal Skeeball value, I wondered? Are they good toward prizes in Seaside? I kept them for years in a desk at home, thinking: "You never know," and eventually forgetting their Skeeball nature. Until they became simply a folded accordian of blank yellow tickets.

One spring I got an invitation to a friend's 10th birthday party. It was written a bit crazily and, I thought happily, what an exciting prospect, Ace's birthday party. Inside was written: "putt putt." I could barely believe his brazenness—a fully-unauthorized reference to smelly uncontrollable low-pitched farting. I laughed my head off. Putt putt. Putt putt.

The day of Ace's birthday, after the cake and the ice cream, we went to Lake City to play miniature golf. On the 18th green, you had to putt into a hole that swallowed up your ball. (No taking your ball and going back to the first hole for you, kid.) The front of the contraption was divided into rectangles offering prizes you could win if they lit up. Free drink. Candy. Free fries. Or the kiss-off. Tough luck. No go. Nix.

When I made out the unlit shadow of the "Free ticket" prize, I said that's what I'm goin' for. I whapped the ball, the lights flashed, and the free ticket sign came on. "Free ticket! I won a free ticket!" I exulted. "I told you that's what I wanted!" I turned and rushed up to the ticket booth. The guy inside had one of those ugly shit-eating grins that one comes to recognize, as he handed me the big ticket.

"It's a free ticket. But it ain't good for anythin'."

"I thought it was for a free game!"

"It doesn't say, 'Free game.' It just says, 'Free ticket.' It's a free ticket. That's all it is. A ticket."

Chapter 6.

Yownskins and the Demonization of Salappa

"She's got really bad breath. If she comes up to correct your paper, man! It's horrible. Yeck! Halitosis!" and Yownskins wrinkled up his nose. Then he was quietly matter-of-fact about how awful Salappa could be.

"She's got a huge mole on her cheek. It's got three bristly black hairs growing out of it. Ugh. And she shaves 'em! Every couple of weeks, suddenly, they're shaved off. Then they start to grow back. Ugh!"

"If she gets pissed, she makes a fist and sticks out her middle knuckle and pounds guys on the shoulders. It really hurts that way. She did it to me once. Or she pinches your shoulder, right there on the tendon. Oww! One time she starts slugging Whitey in the shoulder like that and he starts poking her in the chest with his finger, saying ' Listen, Salappa, you touch me one more time and I'm reportin' you to the School Board.' And she backed off, just kind of shoved him back into the class... Whitey," Yownskins snorted thinking back on how his skinny friend had stood up to Salappa.

"She's got this frizzy red hair. And a bald spot!" said

Yownskins another time. "She's going bald! You can see it when she's bending over to hack up someone's homework!"

"Sup-hose. She wears sup-hose. And her feet are so fat that they are like bulging out of her shoes, the fat is like exploding out of her shoes," exulted Yownskins. "One time Rannem jumped up in class and started making a lot of noise and Salappa grabbed him and tried to shake him around. He just went stiff as a board, and all she could do was slowly tip him back and forth. She was pissed."

There was my introduction to Salappa—she was balding, had bad breath, fetid breath, a hairy mole she shaved with a razor, extremely fat, violent, trained to torture. Known to wear sup-hose, whatever that was. Yownskins is the only person I ever heard speak of it but he usually knew what he was talking about.

Chapter 7.

The Black Rambler

P R N D L. Paranoidal. What the?!

P. (Park.)

Even American Motors is against me.

R. (Reverse.)

Those were the days, when I could turn around and back out. I know where the rockery is, don't have to turn around. Only banged into it once. Raining that time.

N. (Neutral.)

Vasco da Gama was a great man, but he meant nothing to the Finns.

D. (Drive.)

More of the same, that's what's in store for them. That's what they deserve. Little brats, the good for nothings. You're slipping, Knowling. Slip, slips, slip, slipping, slipped. "Keep your eyes on your own paper."

"No talking." I'll give them the business. If they do even the slightest thing, no gym class and no recess. And lunch in the class, while I eat my sandwich, coffee in the thermos. Everyone stays in and does all the optional exercises. Tuna fish tastes better without those little devils laughing and shrieking outside. Business as usual.

L. (Low.)

Parking, reverse, neutral, drive, low. Who's a paranoid, repressed norsewoman, dangerous and loony?! A Salapalolapa loony?

Chapter 8.

Back-To-School Signs

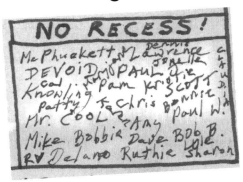

Why do we have to see all those Back-to-School-Sale signs the first second of August? Plastered all over the place? Years later, back-to-school signs began to appear the week after school let out—marketers took the spring out of summer, getting the jump on the fall. I came to dread August. School was looming, imminent, promising interminable reading assignments on crop rotation and fallow fields, promising more of the continuing saga of European explorers slaughtering Indians and colonizing the Americas. Another 300 years looking for the Northwest Passage.

What would grade school have been without recess, or snow that stuck? Everyone would really, truly have run amok. Fuc. They just up and decide to give you Salappa? And that's it?! Why me? I wouldn't wish it on Scudbucket or Lockjaw or Forehead.

Is it any wonder, in retrospect, with teachers' salaries commensurate with those of medieval rat-catchers, that some public schools in Seattle regularly employed psychotic aliens to teach ("to teach")?

Salappa was born March 21, 1907. The last day of winter. In Embarrass, it was still the dead of winter. She had the same birthday as Ovid. And Ibsen.

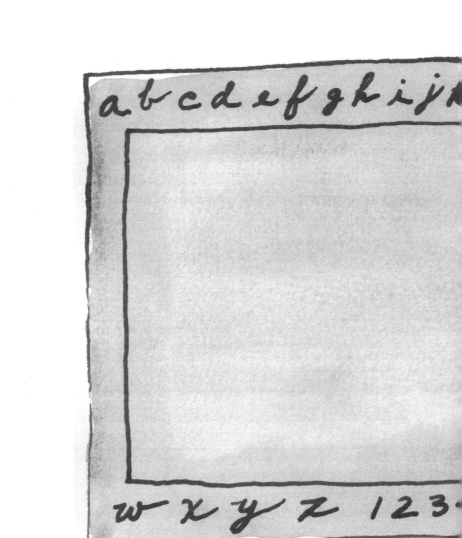

lmnopqrstuv

Fall 1968

NO RECESS!

McPhuckett & Lawrence
DEVOID Paul
Knowling Pam Kristie SCOTT
Patty Chris Bonnie
Mr. COOL Amy Paul W.
Mike Bobbie Dave Bob B.
R. Delano Ruthie Sharon

56789 + - X ÷

Chapter 9.

Sign Language

Day 1. The first week of Salappa's class, Mr. Cool had to sit in the front row and I got to sit about five seats back. Sallappa had it all worked out. Put Coolos right in front of her, so she could sit on him from the start. Another old friend, Devoid, was sitting in front of me. He pleaded with me the first week to put the right answers on his paper when I was correcting it. ("Pass your papers one seat back for corrections.") He'd heard about Her Loppa. Lop lops lop, lopping, lopped. Off.

Coolos and I had planned ahead. We'd worked out a code, something like semaphore, since we were going to be deep behind enemy lines. (Though not as deep as we'd get). That first morning, my friend coughed, then cleared his throat, but not in the genteel, preparatory, loosening "mm mm" manner of my father as he would get up from the dinner table striding to answer the phone. More in an insistent, stage "nnn nnggh!" What? I wondered, pricking up my ears. Without turning around Mr. Cool lifted his right arm slightly and straightened out his forefinger. Of course. Boner at 12 o'clock. Mr. Cool won one round, defying the Sallappic atmosphere of dire consequences. But discreetly. She thought she could control kids—("I'd rather be feared than loved.") And she could—but she couldn't turn our minds inside-out like a pocket. Or keep us from making dirty jokes. The score now stood Coolos 1, Sallappa 1,000. Given her reputation, Salappa had begun with a huge psychological advantage. But we were coming back.

Humor, it's been said, is a consequence of The Fall of Man, eating of the forbidden fruit of the Tree of Knowledge, reason; it's the knowledge or awareness of the difference between what might be and what is; we could be angels, we could be protected and loved by God. But we're not. We've been chased from Eden to survive by the sweat of our brow. Humor is a little compensation, an earthly, earthy form of salvation for humans. It's infuriating to people who demand absolute obedience, to anyone who would be obeyed without question—the authorities: bosses, parents, masters, dictators, police, generals, teachers, Salappa. If they slip on a banana peel or go parading around with no clothes on, someone is going to laugh.

Chapter 10.

Rearranging the Furniture

Every Monday, everyone in Salappa's class had to move their desks to a new spot. One column of kids would move one spot forward. The adjacent columns would move one spot back. The kid in front went to the back of the column. Some kids moved from the front to the back, or the back to the front. This way kids didn't get to stay next to each other and build up any kind of rapport or camaraderie. Kids were always being broken off from their neighbors. Divide and conquer. No ganging up. No revolutionary cells. No joint ventures. No partnerships. When Monday comes, shove your desk like everybody else. Save yourself, if you can. Just you and your desk against the world, in this case, a world ruled by Salappa.

And no one could spend the year hiding in the back of the class. Everyone, sooner or later, had to smell the halitosis.

I was lucky. I started the year at the back of a column of desks that moved forward. Each week I found myself that much closer to Salappa. And one week, there I was, at the front of the column, right in front of her. Every time I looked, I saw this gigantic wart she had on her cheek. And growing out it were three long black hairs. She could easily have been a formidable wench swaggering around in Chaucer's day, drawing considerable attention.

One day at recess, Mr. Cool and I were fantasizing, per usual: "Next time we have to move our desks, let's start pushing the desks forward and then not stop. We'll pen her in and leave her there."

"We'd be dead."

"Yeah, but so would she. It would be worth it, almost."

Chapter 11.

Practical Jokes

Why call jokes "practical?" In my family, pranks were definitely elaborate but never seemed particularly practical. Practical was more like my father smearing on a clown's worth of white lip protector before venturing out into the sun. Or my mother always finishing the leftovers. I guess it's because you put them into practice.

My oldest brother, the Artist-in-residence, was the unrivalled master of the practical joke—the lengthy, secretive process of conceiving a plot, creating the trap, choosing bait, erasing all tracks and traces, and waiting to humiliate the prey. I sometimes wonder where this sadistic comic streak came from? One obvious explanation is that my oldest brother just liked things better before four siblings came rolling in fighting him for space, attention, food, love. His practical jokes were his revenge on the young-and-in-the-way. Or it might simply have been that he too enjoyed what Yownskins once called, rather poetically, "negative delight."

A number of his "jokes" fell under the category of "false generosity." Gumballs filled with pepper and Tabasco. Chocolate chip cookies made with brown crayons. Others were "staged catastrophes" or "false alarms." Furniture not really ruined with disappearing ink. When all was said and done, the overarching ideas were two-fold: "Appearances can be deceiving," and "You blew it, you trusted me."

At the payoff of his practical jokes, when the trap was sprung, the unspoken question was: "Who feels stupid now?" But, that, of course, is implicit in all traps. The goal always was to create the widest disparity between what the victim thinks is going on and what is really going on. The Trojan horse is a good historical precedent.

Chapter 12.

Who Feels Stupid Now?:
The Charles Atlas 14-Day Workout

The tea kettle was beginning to sing. The Artist-in-residence picked up the envelope and held it over the steam, being careful to keep his fingers well out of harm's way. When the glue started to give way, he pried it open a ways, then he held it back in the billowing steam. Two more such maneuvers and it opened.

It was his younger brothers' *Charles Atlas 14-Day Workout*. Ordered from the back of some comic book. ("Hey, quit kicking sand in my eye!") It had just come in the mail. It may have been long awaited, but he felt no need to make its arrival more generally known. Charles Atlas could be improved upon, he was sure of that.

The Artist wanted some time to himself. When no one was around, he spread out the booklet and studied the isometric exercises pictured in the line drawings. Then he took tracing paper and made a few copies. Next he took a stack of clean white paper and began to sketch a few alternative exercises, as useless contortions as possible: "Lie on your stomach and have a partner sit on your back (10 minutes); Bend over, slip your hands under the soles of your feet and lift (10 repetitions of 10 lifts); and using your elbows, point at the ground and the sky at the same time (5 repetitions, alternating elbows). While wearing a pair of hiking boots, pull yourself up by your bootstraps. If the shoelaces break, replace, and begin again."

He typed up fake instructions for each of the exercises ("particularly good for the gluteous maximal muscles." "Helps tone the noodle oblongata.")

He took his drawings and instructions and made Xerox copies of them, so they'd look printed. He put his handiwork back in the original Charles Atlas envelope and sealed it with Elmer's glue. When the mail came, he slipped it in with the rest of the pile.

His younger brothers, Hade and Yownskins, were quite excited to see Charles Atlas had come for them in the mail. (Who wants to be a 98-lb. weakling?!) They ripped it open, pored over the precious information, and began a regular, strenuous regimen of isometric exercise. After a couple of weeks of laughing to himself, the Artiste flipped them the original book of beefcake recipes, and let them in on the joke.

Brains, he was clearly saying, will always triumph over brawn. Charles Atlas soon languished in a dresser drawer. Hey, they never really planned on becoming beach bums anyway. In Seattle, no sun, no beach.

Chapter 13.

Recess in the Covered Playcourt

In Seattle, school begins in September, the first Wednesday after Labor Day. The first week only lasts from Wednesday to Friday, a three-day week. A three-day week to ease into the school year, the next nine months. Some years the rain began even earlier—in mid-August—and seemed to go until April, only to start up again in June. The days would get colder, wetter, and darker as winter came. A typical winter day: 37 degrees and raining. Not quite cold enough to snow, but cold enough to freeze your balls off.

"It's colder than a witch's tit."

"It's colder than Salappa's butt."

Recess on rainy days was spent in the "playcourt," a concrete room with a high, corrugated metal roof, low concrete walls, and a heavy wire fence that stretched from the top of the walls to the roof. A few dim lights protected in wire cages hung from the ceiling. The playcourt had two doorways that opened out onto the playground and two sets of double doors that opened back into the school—the boys' lavatory and the girls' lavatory.

Recess in the covered playcourt was a poor excuse

for freedom. All the kids wearing raincoats and galoshes even though we couldn't go out in the rain. I usually stood up against a wall and watched classmates who seemed to be having fun. I didn't get it. You could bring red rubber balls into the playcourt for bouncing or soak 'em. There were the small ones that could be bounced off a friend's head and only cause minor neck sprain or a scalp burn. There were slightly larger balls that could be thrown with accuracy and would sting if they caught you square on. And there were one or two huge rubber balls that were no good to throw but were great to kick. A good solid kick would send them into a concrete wall and flatten them with a funny splat that would crack and boom like a thunderclap. From time to time, like cymbals, a kicked ball would clang off a caged light.

Some days, when the rain fell in sheets, we could look through the fence of the playcourt and watch the water blown in waves, running first one direction then back again, and the sky would turn dark and gray as wet concrete. Most of the rain in Seattle was what my mother called a "drizzle," hardly any wind, small raindrops in no particular hurry.

A real downpour grabbed one's attention. Safe and warm at home, I liked to put my nose up close to a cold window and watch the back stairs become a river, watch the puddles jump. I loved the sound of the percussion build to its crescendo, doubling its vehemence. I knew it couldn't keep it up, that the rain would soon stop.

In Sallappa's class you weren't supposed to look out

the window. An occasional glance at the rain was enough to know that there wasn't much to look at anyway, not much to look forward to outside. Days on end were accompanied by the somber sound of the rain's monotonous music.

Sometimes everyone in the covered playcourt would stop as the rain suddenly rushed down twice as hard as it had, the snare drum rhythm beating on the metal roof and the drops scattering, wind-dashed across the deserted concrete playground. There's something oppressive and exhilarating about the sound of a real storm, the rain getting even worse. Now it was sure that they wouldn't be able to go outside later. They'd probably get soaked on the way home. No playing outside after school.

Penned in. Pent up. We all roared with the rain's melancholy and exploded in a frenzied, unchoreographed dance of war. A hundred kids. Bedlam. The running, the shrieking, rubber balls blasting, all squeezed into a concrete pen wrapped in rain. In the muddy, muddled, unintelligible pandemonium, I put my fingers to my ears, and tapped openshutopenshutopenshut, breaking the noise into doo-wah-doo-wah-wah-wah-wah-wah-wah.

Most kids ran in circles, giggling, knocking each other down, threatening to trample each other. Around and around they'd go. In the confusion, there was always one clear lonely sight: a ball bouncing through one of the open doorways into the thrashing skeins of rain, bounding unchased across the empty playground, rolling to the far fence. And there was always the

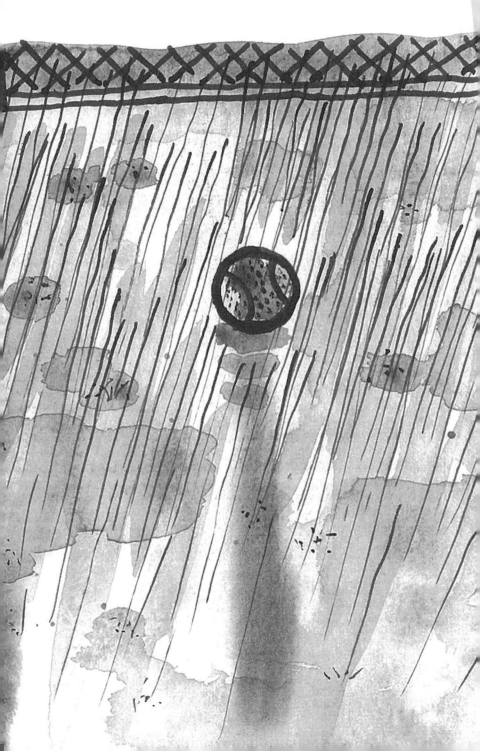

question: who's the sucker who has to get it? Who threw it at the broad side of the playcourt and missed?

You could use those days in the covered playcourt to get a small idea of the pressures people feel in crowds, huge cities, how tempers snap, how inhuman it is to live where there's only concrete, tar, cement, asphalt—no grass, no trees, no shrubbery, no parking strips. Where urban renewal means cutting down blocks of trees—so there are fewer places for muggers to hide. How violence is inevitable and the only sane reaction is to run, or keep your back to the wall, ready to dodge left or right.

Or you could use the time to imagine a prison yard, how you got out—kind of—for a little while to stretch your limbs, but you were still caged in, what it's like to have only the option of moving from one cage to another. You could have studied mass hysteria, how you shouldn't yell "fire!" in a crowded theater, how you shouldn't trip little kids, or knock your friends down as they're trying to get out of a burning building.

When the bell blared sending us back to class, the double doors to the lavatories were hauled open, and fifteen of us toppled through them onto the floor, just inside the school, yelling "pig pile!" This was the high point of a rainy recess—sabotage—and the chance to dash the hope any teacher might have had of an orderly return to class. "Pig pile!"

The playground teacher would stand over us—a laughing, screaming, squirming mass on the floor—shouting for us to get up, meanwhile more kids flopped on top. It was one way of letting teachers know that we still had enough tricks and energy to last the rest of the day. Pig piles were a crime of passive, antic resistance, a conspiracy meant to look like an accident. No one could be held responsible, certainly not the poor guy on the bottom. He was the cause in a way, but most likely he'd been tripped or shoved, tackled from behind without the ball.

It was also a transgression that could be plausibly denied. "We fell down!" "I was pushed!" Finally we would scramble back to our feet laughing and hustle back to class. In thirty seconds it was over, a thirty-second orgy to revive the spirits. Even better than a nap.

Chapter 14.

Rain

Eskimos, with their all their names for snow, have nothing on Seattleites and our many ways to describe liquid sunshine.

In Seattle, we often say that it's drizzling. Just a little drizzle. Or it's sprinkling. Just raining a little bit. There's a fine mist, silent and miraculous fine. (Imagine single water molecules settling over the city.) It's damp. It's damp out. A little precipitation. A little precip. First it rains then it drips... unexpected drops off the leaves, off the telephone wires, and plunk, down the back of your neck.

A light rain. Light showers. Intermittent showers. Heavy showers. Driving rain. Sleet. Rain mixed with snow. The snow won't last. They say it's going to turn to rain. It's not sticking. A violent rainstorm. Not Seattle's type of fun (typhoon). Thunder and lightning, cracking and rumbling. We had an inch of rain last night. It was really coming down. Freezing rain.

It's starting to rain in earnest. It's raining steadily. It isn't letting up. It's been raining non-stop for days. Nothing but rain. It's raining constantly. We got rained on. The wettest Fall-Winter-Spring-and-Summer on

record. The wettest year ever. Wettest decade ever recorded. Need we go on? We're at sea in Seattle, see?'
It's pouring. It's pouring down. It's pissing rain. We had a real downpour. A pelting rain. Rain is beating down, drumming on the windows. Raindrops fell like pearls from a snapped necklace. It's coming down hard. Sheets of rain. We got soaked. We got drenched. We got sopping wet. Everything got waterlogged. Leave your wet things at the back door.

Clouds. The clouds are ready to burst. Rain clouds. It's cloudy. It's overcast. We have a thick cloud covering over much of Western Washington. We'll be socked in through the weekend with perhaps some clearing on Monday. It's gray. Looks like a gray day. The sky is gray. Ashen. But it doesn't look like it's going to rain. It's raining across the lake. You can tell. The clouds are smeared down to the ground. Like sharp chalk lines rubbed partly away by an artist's thumb.

The particle/wave theory of Seattle—the raindrop/puddle continuum—everywhere you step is an optics experiment. Caught between rain's stalactites and stalagmites, water pouring down and water splashing up. Between heaven and earth, wet heads and wet pants. Negative space.

The Killjoy sneered at anyone who wore his blue jeans rolled up. Those were known as "rain gauges," as if the kid was gathering rainfall data. It really meant their parents were probably trying to buy them clothes that were three sizes too big so they would last through a growing spurt, several years growing. Or that they were wearing hand-me-downs. Rain gauges were about as cool as a pig shave or black high-tops. Or salt-and-pepper cords.

So many shades of gray. So many layers of clouds. Behind one, endless others. A black-and-white photographer's paradise—life on a gray-scale. Contrast and its negating background of white. The gun metal gray clouds turn Puget Sound black, Lake Washington dark gray, Green Lake slate. The playground's the color of #2 pencil lead. Gray shaded blue, like a fresh dye job. It looks like rain.

Sometimes, as if by magic, the clouds slide by so fast that the earth feels as if it's turning under your feet. The clouds wheeling overhead.

Look at all the fog! It's really foggy. It's dewy. Condensation. People are mildewing. It's misty. Dank. Thank you, achoo. It's wet out. Bundle up. It's cold and wet. Moldy. Like a moldering grave, but you get used to it. Rain's inevitability breeds a certain Seattle stoicism.

"God is all wet with rain." It just keeps falling. The rain's not letting up. It's been raining for months. It's February and it's been raining like this since mid-September. When it doesn't rain during school, for a change it rains on the weekend.

A perverse fact of life in Seattle: it's usually sunny in April and May. Then when school gets out in June, it starts raining again. Always rains for Chanukah and Christmas. The Evergreen state. Ever wet. Everwet the Unruddy.

Once it was raining and the sun had just gone down behind the Olympic Mountains and like an arc-lamp it still burned one thin strip of a cloud a blinding white, a molten tear in the clouds, white-hot right on the horizon. That's right. Right as rain.

The newspapers label some Seattle weather PC—not politically correct but partly cloudy—which makes no sense. In Seattle, if it's partly cloudy, it means you can see some blue sky. That's sunny! That's a sunny day! If the sun breaks through the clouds for one second in the day, that's some sunshine, man. That's a sunny day! If you see a rainbow, the sun's got to be out! Sheesh, that's practically a sunny day... in Seattle.

Chapter 15.

Negative Space

Salappa's vibrations were something like infinite "negative space," competing for dominance over the universe's rambunctious impulsive flights of giddyup.

The long arm of nothing. A total old-school hardass. A tsunami of fat and fury. Maybe she was a good person, really, in reality. Let's face it. She dedicated her life to teaching. Never missed a day! Another teacher told me years later that they were paid so poorly and with no sick leave pay that she could believe it when I said I thought Sallappa never missed a day.

When Salappa is alone, I imagine her entering her house and her flabby exterior dropping onto the floor. Her skeleton walks over and hangs itself on a coat rack. Right over where she checked her heart on the way out. Then her negative interior is unloosed, a black silt that whirls through the house like sulphur or volcanic dust. The air in her house smells like asphalt. A couple of kids try to save her from the fire they think is spreading through her house. But, when they open the door, a hound of blackest hell chaws on them. All that's left: a half-eaten brown-and-white saddleshoe.

Whenever we laid eyes on a black Rambler, even if

Sullapa wasn't behind the wheel, Mr. Cool would fall on the ground and roll around in agony. Other wiseacres did likewise.

One night, years later, I dreamt that I was studying Sallapa and I remember thinking specifically that it was like working in a science lab with an oversized guinea pig. After a little while, I started to get an uneasy feeling, having her within lunging distance. I told her she could go now, but she said something, that woke me with a jolt of terror.

She said: "No. I won't."

Chapter 16.

All that was Left of Chatty Cathy

One rainy day, walking home from school, Yownskins and I found the frowzy, muddy head of a decapitated Chatty Cathy doll lying in a puddle. Our sister had one. It was her favorite doll. Struck with a bright idea, we hid her real doll and left this Medusa head on her bed.

When she saw it, she screamed as if her leg had been ripped off at the knee. The walls bulged, large patches of the lawn withered, windows chattered. We tried to calm her down. Our mother came rushing upstairs to find us frantically thrusting her real doll into her arms.

"Chatty Cathy!" our sister blubbered.

"Boys! How could you do such a thing?!"

"It was just a joke," said my older brother.

A classic. No permanent harm done. An off-the-scale overreaction. The victim suffered once, and then later could be reminded how she'd been fooled, how dumb she'd been. How dumb she'd forever be, as long as there was memory.

Chatty Cathy had a tape loop inside and a string that you pulled to make her "talk." Toy makers have made

great advances since then. Years later, I pulled the string on a talking Mr. T doll and it growled: "Always obey your parents!"

Chapter 17.

The School Carnival

Maybe they'll work at the school carnival! I wonder, I wonder. Might as well bring them along, I thought, as I shoved the string of yellow Skeeball tickets down to the bottom of my pocket. It was carnival night. One night around Halloween, the school penitentiary would be wildly cheered up with a carnival. Everyone would come home in the afternoon and then go back to school in the evening and it would be dark out and raining and then all of a sudden we'd push open the heavy doors and find ourselves in the middle of a mob, hubbub, excitement, and chaos—costumes, contests, and popcorn balls. The normal school regimentation—walking in straight lines, not talking with one's neighbor—was overthrown for the night. For once we poured into the school, oldsters and youngsters, and shrieked and yelled and played tag and shoved kids into the lockers with big bangs.

And if you could produce blank yellow tickets, you could go into the different classrooms designed and decked out for fun and games. One room housed a "white elephant," advertised by a hulking elephant painted on a bedsheet. I peeked inside and saw throngs of mothers picking through boxes of clothing. And yet I couldn't dispel the notion that there was something illicit and racy about a white elephant. Pink elephants, white elephants? If I gave them a Skeeball ticket would I come weaving back out with white elephants dancing in my head? But I knew I was too young. I couldn't have stood getting turned away at the door or the dirty look of some parent.

So I followed my nose toward the sweets. The halls were filled with the smell of cotton candy, popcorn balls, caramel apples, ambrosia. Helium balloons jounced against each other like zeppelins at rush hour. Gone were the usual smells—chalk dust, crayons, meat blanquette. Maybe it wasn't a penitentiary after all. Why were we doing penance anyway? For the sin of being little kids?

I didn't ever remember feeling like a kid. From the time I went to kindergarten and was aware of talking to myself in my head, silently, not moving my lips, I felt like myself, small, but not like some halfwit, some kid.

I bought a helium balloon and was walking it down the crowded hall closing in fast on a man calmly stirring sugar into billowing layers of cotton candy, the air sweet, alive with excited voices, when outta the balloo I heard my balloon go kaballoom. Shit, I thought, I just got that.

Then I saw a couple of twelve-year-old hoods laughing and saw them use a pin to pop a little girl's balloon. She began screaming bloody murder. They slipped away smiling, death's apprentices; it takes so little coaxing, a little tickling for the plastic to give up the ghost, for the helium to shred its skin. Imagine those hoods' surprise when they have to spend eternity getting pricked with pins by hysterical balloonless kids.

Late in the evening of the Carnival they would show films. They'd set up a classroom with folding chairs and then kids and adults would play musical chairs and the hapless and the overly timid or polite spectators would sit on a counter or line the walls. Outside the classroom in the hallway, people were getting their hands painted red by somebody's Mom. She was supposed to be a gypsy. "Palms read," her sign red. Luckily I saw a red palm before I gave her one of my Skeeball tickets. I'd been tempted to lay down some good chit.

Inside some of the younger teachers were singing and dancing, decked out as flappers, shivering in their silky fringe in the cool room, waving ostrich boa wraps lightly around themselves, kicking and laughing before a blackboard. "The Roaring Twenties." They were spirited, definitely worth the price of admission. Why didn't I get that pretty sweet young blonde teacher for my teacher? That's what I wanted to know. If you had a fresh popcorn ball or two to nibble on, that was a fun night.

After the flappers had shimmied off to their undressing rooms, someone caught the lights and turned on the movie projector. As I was gnawing off a big hunk of sweet popcorn, and Buster Keaton was careening around corners and down alleys, trying to outrun the Keystone Kops, Mr. Cool hopped up on the counter next to me. Somehow he spotted me in the flickering black-and-white light, hiding behind a partially-eaten popcorn ball. I was distracted watching the chase through the sugary strands of the sticky popcorn and I began to tear another chunk off. I watched as the sugar attenuated from crystalline threads to hairs to the finest filament, no more than a molecule wide, finally snapping and floating hardening upward... Coolos tapped me and whispered: "Vis. Look what I found."

He held out his hand, trying to give me something. With my hands clasped around not one but two popcorn balls (one half eaten), I wasn't quick to take what Coolos offered. I looked around for a spot to put down one of the sticky balls, but being hemmed in on both sides by other filmgoers, I finally rested the untouched popcorn ball on my knee. "It won't pick up too much lint if I set it down lightly," I thought to myself. I put out a gummy hand and he laid something shiny in it. It felt almost mechanical. As I turned it around in my palm, it caught the light of Buster Keaton's pale, forlorn expression and I realized that I was holding an old-fashioned pair of women's pointy glasses.

As I was staring at them, I felt Coolos lift the popcorn ball off my knee and heard him crunch into it.

"Help yourself."

"Try 'em on."

"Later."

"They're Sullappa's."

I laughed. Another crack. "Did you find your glasses?"

"No! Really, they're..."

A heavy hand came down on my shoulder. "Either you boys pipe down or you're going to have to leave. Other people are trying to watch the movie. Is that clear?" Some teacher. My insides were already jumping with the thought of holding Salapa's specs, but when I heard that voice in my ear, I dissolved like crayons on a cookie sheet. I nodded, keeping my knees clenched together until I saw the teacher lower himself back into his folding chair. When his face once again was flickering peacefully with the tribulations of Buster Keaton, I jabbed Mr. Cool with the pointed corner of Supalup's glasses. I didn't want them on me a second longer. As I slipped them into a discreetly proffered hand, I knocked the popcorn ball off my knee. Like a little bunny it hopped to the floor and scampered into a thicket of feet and folding chairs. Our luck was already changing. When I looked back, Coolos was leaning toward me and shaking his head like one of those dashboard baseball players with its head bobbing on a spring. He was wearing Sowlipup's glasses, sticking his tongue out and leering.

A truly horrible sight. The film ran off the reel, and someone threw the lights on while the juvenile linguists

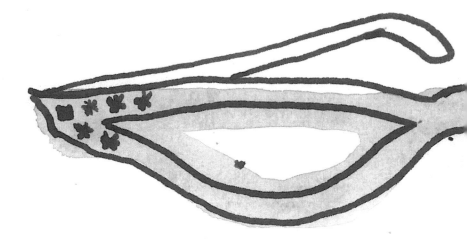

began debating the pronunciation of "the" in "the end." Was it a long "e" or a short "e"? Back and forth they screamed thuh end! thee end! thuh end! thee end! Amidst the swelling intellectual discourse, a dialectic incapable of synthesis (unless there exists a medium "e," as in, "they end"), amidst a roomful of kids calling for the cosmic period, howling for surcease from grade school (what else did we know?) rose the authorities, Roscoe, Malluck, and Crewcut looking for malefactors.

And there were Sollypop's glasses sparkling on the bridge of my friend's nose. "Let's get out of here," I hissed. We were right next to the door. Fortunately. Mr. Cool slid off the counter and without taking off the skyblue rhinestone-encrusted glasses, he bolted between two bulky parents and out the door. The gap between the overstuffed limegreen stretchpants and the underfilled beige mackintosh was quickly closing. "S'cuse me," I muttered as I squeezed through the fleshy gates.

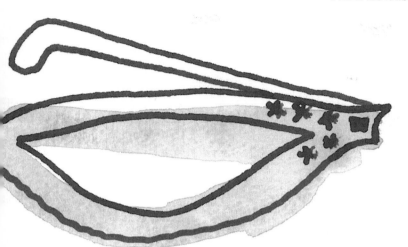

In the hall I saw my friend throwing his shoulder against one of the doors out of the building. It didn't open. He threw himself against the other one and it banged open and he fell out on his hands and knees. He jumped up and I sprinted after him out into the rain. We'd excaped by the peachfuzz of our chinny chin chins.

"C'mon, Vis," my friend called as he scrambled across the playground, saddle shoes flying. We tore across the dark expanse of "the lowers" and then down countless stairs to the gloom of "the lowerlowers." By the time we reached the lowerlowers we were gasping for breath and giggling hysterically. The playfield was like a rice paddy during the monsoons, all mud and lakes.

"Think they're following us?"

"Shhh."

"I don't hear anything."

"Quick, let's wait behind the backstop. If we see someone coming, we run for it."

"We got out of there fast! But I think Crewlbutt saw you."

"They were my grandmother's."

"Yeah?"

"No."

"So, tell!"

"I picked the lock with a bobbypin."

"That only works on TV."

"I'm not kidding. I stuck a hairpin in the lock, twisted it as hard as I could and Sullapa's door opened."

"God."

"So I went in to take a look around."

"Jesus."

"I got goose pimples all over standing there."

"Goose bumps?"

"Yeah. My neckhair stood up like crazy. I thought for a second she was sitting at her desk. I almost blurted out sorry I forgot my homework, I hope it isn't too late to turn it in."

"She wouldn't of believed that in a zillion years."

"Well, if that hadn't worked, I was ready to fight her hand-to-hand combat."

"Shesus. She's a strong muthuh."

"You know that social studies test from last week? I got an E on it."

"Oof."

"It's no big whoop. I figgered I'd give myself a B+ if I could find her grade book. She's got all those red pens; it wouldn't have been that hard to fake. Just round off the E and add a +. But all the desk drawers were locked, except one that had a bunch of red pens and these glasses."

"You took 'em?!"

"Peanutbuttuhmahn strikes again! I left her a snowcone for a trade."

"Really?"

"Haha, fooled you, Vis. I left a tack on her chair."

"Come on..."

"No kiddin'. Wish we could watch her find it."

"Oh, God, Sulluppa sitting on a big, fat tack. I'm glad we won't be there!"

"Let's go. No one's comin'."

"Yeah, let's go."

We slogged the length of the flooded lowerlowers hugging the north fence and the shadows. As we paused on the hill overlooking the public playfield below, Mr. Cool pulled out the glasses.

"Try 'em on. They're weird."

"Okay."

I unfolded the glasses and slipped them on. The tips of the metal earpieces cut into my ears. And the coke bottle lenses bent the world around and back on itself. I felt as if my eyes would leap out of their sockets or that my head would cave in. I squeezed my eyes shut and ripped them off.

"Horrible."

"I can see pretty good with 'em."

"Uh-oh, look. Your pants."

"Sheeit! It's musta been when I fell through the door, and they're brand new! My parents are gonna kill me! Ripped with blood on 'em. My mom's gonna love that."

"You couldn't help it..."

"There's only one hope: go in the back, sneak upstairs and change into my p.j.'s. Then pray."

Chapter 18.

The Flux of Life

A few days after the Carnival, I stopped over at Coolos' house. When I came into his second story room on the southwest corner of the barracks, he was sitting on the floor with his back against his bed and Solapa's glasses on his nose.

"Omigod!"

"You're slipping Knowling!"

"Sheesh."

"There is no noise in Illinois!"

"Snap out of it!"

"Mad doesn't mean angry. It means crazy!"

"Cut it out!"

"Now take out your two-ton social studies text. I want you to do all the exercises at the back of Chapter IX for tomorrow—all of A,B,C, and D—and all of the optional exercises!"

I couldn't stand the idea of The Syko taking over my friend. I pulled the glasses off Mr. Cool, who started to laugh and rub his eyes.

"That's really weird, Vis."

"You're not kiddin'."

"I figger if I wear her glasses long enough, I'll maybe figger out why she's such a mean fuccer."

"Just don't let her take you over."

"Wanta try 'em on?"

"No way! That's supposed to be bad for your eyes, to wear someone else's prescription. That's what my mom says."

"I wouldn't believe everything your mom says. "Remember when she told you sex was called 'fertilization?'"

"So what? 'Sexual intercourse' isn't much better."

"Intercourse."

"It's in my dad's unabridged dictionary. Big dic. I looked it up. There's also something called 'social intercourse.' It's supposed to mean talking."

"Talking dirty."

"Let's tell Sullupa we want to have social intercourse with her."

"Gross."

"No kiddin'."

"I hope you have seven kids."

"I hope you have ten. You'd have to do it ten times!"

"I'm never gettin' married."

"Did your parents tell you about the birds and the bees?"

"The who's and the what's?"

"The birds and the bees. Mine did, but who cares about birds and bees?"

"They don't tell me anything. Go ask your parents some more and report back."

"I'm never gettin' married. But you are and you're gonna have a dozen kids!"

"Not me. I'm never gettin' married. But you are. You're gonna have a hundred kids."

"Gross!"

Chapter 19.

Mad vs. Crazy

Getting mad and going mad. Getting crazy and going crazy. Eating nuts and going nuts.

"Mad doesn't mean angry," Salapa said angrily, talking her usual craziness. "Mad means crazy." The kids in her class exchanged puzzled, disgusted looks. Here was another of Sulapa's dumb aphorisms. She could repeat them as often as she liked, that still wouldn't convince us. I mean, what the heck?! Mad doesn't mean mad?? Since when?

When we all objected simultaneously, and I jumped up and grabbed a dictionary, Salopa went a little insane, defending her definition of mad, a ridiculously common member of the lingua franca.

"It says under the fourth definition that mad can mean extremely angry," I read in a loud voice.

"Let me see that," she commanded.

Rearranging herself on the front of her battered desk, Salopa's lips moved as she read the dictionary. Her sup-hose shifted irritably as we waited for her to admit that the whole world wasn't wrong.

"It says right here under the first entry: 'Suffering from a mental disorder; insane.' That's the correct meaning and anyone using the word mad to mean angry in my class or in written assignments will have their grade knocked down." You should have seen the look on her face when G told her that his older brother made him mad, because he'd told on him and his parents had gotten mad at him, and the dumb thing was it wasn't anything to get mad about anyway. I had never seen a frown seem to bend in three directions at once before, but there it was, smiling with revenge in mind.

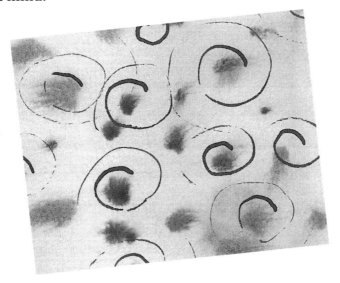

Chapter 20.

The World's Biggest Idiots

One day Miss Salappa looked at her regulation dark green waste basket and started into a slow boil.

"Look at all the paper you kids are wasting. This is a disgrace. I bet you've hardly written on this paper before throwing it away. I'm going to go through this right now...." She picked up the garbage can and took it to her desk and she started pulling out sheets of school-issued writing paper, a light tan paper with light blue lines printed on it. Nobody could breathe.

There were only a few scribbles on the first few sheets. Next she pulled out one sheet and she stared at it for a long time. Then she jumped up, her face flushed, and she said: "Girls. I've got to talk to the boys alone. I want you all to get up right this instant and go out into the hall. Wait there until I come get you." The girls looked around a bit puzzled and then got up and hustled out of the classroom, quietly, excitedly, not daring even a whisper.

Then Salappa turned to us guys and said: "Boys, someone in this class has written something very, very bad. None of you is leaving until I find out who it was." With that she took the piece of paper she was crunching in her hand and taped it to the blackboard. "I want you to take a look at it, and then whoever did this, well, if you know what's good for you, you better confess."

Row by row she let the boys come up to the board to inspect the paper, which read, in extremely legible cursive writing: "Fuc you Sallabutt." And below that it had several teachers' names, including Salappa's, arranged under the heading: "World's Biggest Idiots." You couldn't have cut the atmosphere in the classroom with a machete. I felt ill.

After they'd all had a chance to inspect the offending paper, they sat staring at their desks and at each other in brief sidelong glances, the deathly silence of the condemned. Some guys thought this was hilarious, guys who weren't about to get Sallopaed.

"All right! Who's the smart aleck? Which one of you wrote this?" No one said a thing. "Do any of you recognize the handwriting? If you do, tell me right now who's work this is." Silence. "You're not leaving this classroom until I find the culprit!"

Then Salappa had an idea. She took a stack of blank paper and began handing out one sheet to each boy. "Okay, I want you to copy what's written on that note. I'm going to get to the bottom of this, one way or another!" This was too good to be true—an assignment they could really put their heart into. Dutifully, they each wrote the offending word with a "k." When she collected them, she only found one without a "k." Mine. She came up to my desk and snarled: "All right,

Knowling," and she grabbed my arm and yanked me to my feet.

I wanted to cry but I was basically suffering an emotional brain freeze as she dragged me out of the class. She grabbed the tendon in my shoulder and pinched me using the death grip of the Finnish Inquisition. She gripped me like that all the way down the hall to the principal's office. I thought she was going to kill me. That was the most memorable spelling lesson I ever had.

Chapter 21.

The Tintinnabulation of the Bells

The school day was filled with bells, bells, bells, bells, bells. As Edgar Allan Poe put it: "The tintinnabulation of the bells." The 9:00 tardy bell. The 10:30 recess bell. The freeze bell. The walk bell. The tardy bell. The lunch bell. The freeze bell. The walk bell. The tardy bell. The fire-drill bell. The imminent nuclear holocaust bell. The earthquake bell. The 1:30 recess bell. The freeze bell. The walk bell. The tardy bell. The 3:00. 3:05. 3:08. 3:10 thank-god-school's-over bell that put us one day closer to the summer-vacation-at-long-last-bell.

The freeze bell served as a game of statue-maker for crowds. We were supposed to freeze and hold the position we happened to be in when the honking began. We were supposed to try and catch our arms to keep from throwing that bloated red rubber ball blatchkaplatch off a flat concrete wall or the heels of a kickball scrambler motoring for third. All at once hundreds of kids were trying to hold up. To stop a jump rope in full revolution or a tetherball in full career. A four-square slam spinning past square one. Or Coolos and me rattling the chainlink fence.

Recess was the high point of every day. Most everything worth knowing I learned at recess. Fifteen minutes in the morning. An hour for lunch. Fifteen minutes in the afternoon. This was real life in all its variety. To most teachers, recess was an unalienable right. To Saloppa it was a privilege that could easily be forfeited.

Early on Salapa explained with grim pleasure that she kept a square of the blackboard free for the names of little boys and girls who did not follow the rules. Kids who had to go to the lavatory during class instead of during recess when they were supposed to had to put their names on the board and make up the time later. (Making up the time meant sitting in her stifling cheerless presence during recess, lunch, or after school.) Kids who forgot their homework met the same end. Kids who talked, kids who laughed, kids who farted, kids who were late. Everyday lots of kids had to write their names into the square in the corner of the blackboard. It was always jammed with our names.

Everyday we were deprived of recess, gym, lunch, Life after school—the day's only unalloyed pleasures— instead having to make up the time sitting in Sallappa's class doing optional exercises at the back of the chapter of some beat textbook. Some wrote their names big, others microscopically, all in weary misery.

Chapter 22.

Lunchtime Kickball

If recess had the sweet taste of freedom, lunch hour was an entire meal. Stepping outside the brick compound of our elementary school was what crossing the river Lethe must have been like: one's boredom, fears, and regrets, that ragtag outfit that each of us fashions for himself, is shed in the warm, cool waves of a mercurial sea, a torrent that might have been made from a million broken thermometers, a dreaming stream that swiftly unweaves our lives' brocade and leaves us stripped of care to gambol in the Elysian fields, or in our case, atop the playgrounds—the so-called "lowers" and "lowerlowers."

Lunch period seemed to spread out infinitely with kickball diamonds, backstops, broad walls, tetherballs, basketball hoops, and scores of red rubber balls. Kids used to race to finish eating lunch first (or throwing it into garbage cans first), because in kickball, the first, second, and third to touch homeplate got to kick first. Everyone else had to start in the field. The late-comers had to get someone out—catch a kicked ball on the fly or hit a base runner rambling between bases—to get the chance to kick the heck out of that red rubber ball.

It was a lot easier to skip lunch and tag home plate while other kids were still scarfing down their Hostess Ho-ho's.

Usually it went something like this. We would sit down in the auditorium to eat. We would look at the school lunch. We would look at each other. We would quickly look for the authorities. Then all at once, we would shove our chairs back with a screech, hustle over to the garbage cans, dump a gluey mountain of chicken chow mein, and then we would speedwalk as fast as we could past the hall monitors to the boys' lavatory, sprint to the double doors to the playcourt, bang them open and begin the all-out fifty-yard dash for the far side of the playground and home plate. One, two, three. Slap slap slap went our tennis shoes. Pitcher! First base! While waiting for the outfield to eat their lunches and come play, I would catch my breath, savor the privilege of kicking second, shake the chainlink fence, feel the sun on my face, and forget all about Salappa and Social Studies.

Kickball is one of the world's great games. The pitcher would roll the ball toward the kicker, trying to get it to cross home plate. The kicker got to take a short run to kick the ball, which more often than not was a medium industrial-strength red rubber job.

A few guys excelled at catching line drives. Holco liked to pitch because he was a fearless defensive wizard. He could take a colossal blast in the chest and hold on. Sometimes the force of the shot would actually knock him off his feet. Other times he would stand there like a concrete wall and clutch at the ball exploding off his chest, then clutch again, but it would get away and he even might dive for it as it sank to the ground. And whether he caught that one or not, the sound and the courage were duly noted and everyone laughed and nodded in disbelief.

Some people excelled at kicking rubber balls. One big, fat black kid regularly kicked long fly balls that would sail over the outfield fence. That too was impressive, almost superhuman in fact, but it was also almost understandable. The guy was twice the size of the rest of us.

Then there was a motley collection of kids who had strong throwing arms and were fairly merciless. Here would come some hapless runner rounding second, heading full-bore for third when he'd get nailed by a great throw, hammered right at the ankles. His legs would get slammed together and the poor guy would go flipping through the air onto the concrete. It was funny if he didn't break anything. Otherwise kids would crowd around and console the winged warrior, help him up, or if it were serious, take him to the nurse's office.

Chapter 23.

Saturday Downtown

The WAC. The Whack. Mr. Cool was a member of the Washington Athletic Club. And much to my surprise, so was I. Both of us had beat-up orange membership cards that testified to our privilege and athleticism. We were junior members, and we took the bus downtown and went there on our own, which made us feel a bit like real members, free to roam floors one, two, and eight.

One time we decided to explore a little farther afield. We tested the waters by going to the men's locker-room on the sixth floor, usually off-limits to kids. Coolos insisted, leading the way past a number of old men to a counter where you could order drinks.

"You gotta try this gator drink they have."

"Alligator drink?"

There in back were a bunch more old guys lolling around fat and pink and naked. One was getting a massage. I tried not to look. Some had towels around their waists, some were just sitting there in the nude with great sweeping bellies and quiescent wieners. No boners there.

We bought two alligator somethings in dixie cups. It turned out to be a greenish liquid that was salty, exotic, and terrible tasting. But it was interesting, and not a little daunting, to walk on into the old codgers' inner sanctum. Not only had we gone where few little punks go, but the elevator we took stopped on other floors that were forbidden, suggesting unknown, hidden pleasures. More exciting transgressions. One floor was even called the penthouse.

"Which floor is the women's locker-room?"

"Wonder if we can get some gator juice there?"

Considering how quickly we found ourselves in the men's locker-room, we wondered if maybe the elevator would open by chance on some other floor and we would find ourselves in the middle of the women's locker-room. Maybe the sight of two little boys would be such a welcome change that they would invite us in, give us massages, hide us from the club's secret police, and make us miss our bus.

We tried the basement next. We pressed "B" in the elevator and waited. When the door chugged open, we discovered another old-fashioned folding metal gate that had to be slid aside. Beyond that was the sign for a subterranean bar, hidden around the corner. We took a couple of steps out of the elevator but lost our nerve. What if the elevator left without us?

As the elevator started to close, we jumped back in laughing our butts off, but before the doors could close, a mean-looking man stepped in with us. Our smiles vanished. He looked us up and down. "You boys lost?"

he asked accusingly. "Uh, yeah, we were looking for the bowling alley." "You're not going to find it sneaking around the basement." "We thought that's what the B stood for." We both stared at the floor in the elevator, waiting to get the hell away from that guy. When the elevator finally came to rest back in the lobby, he said: "After you, boys," and we hustled out.

Chapter 24.

Falling

Bored, I looked cautiously around the classroom. I'd noticed her before, but there and then, for the first time, I felt my eyes turning back to her, I didn't care which explorer was looking for the Northwest Passage, everything was better if I could just glance at her every so often.

She wore her dark hair medium short, and she had a dancing way of running when we were outside playing. She even had a pretty good arm, though she didn't seem to care much for soak 'em one way or another. When she smiled or laughed, you could see she had lost one of her eyeteeth and was waiting for it to grow back in.

I felt a pang, some sort of dart. She was sitting between Devoid and McPhuckett, not doing anything special, sucking on the end of her pencil and staring at the ceiling. I began to fall in love with her, the dancing dark-haired girl with the missing eyetooth. It was as if I could only turn away from her for a second before I had to look back. It was good but not good. Infatuation comes from fatuous (i.e., foolish or even idiotic). A crush. Love crushes both ways—outcrushlonging and incrushdrumming—and both ways it hurts.

Chapter 25.

The World's Fastest Human Plays Dodgeball

I was standing in the middle of the playground wondering which way to turn. Games were everywhere, but I couldn't decide which to play. Some were already in full swing, some were for girls. The girl with the dark hair was playing tetherball. I'd once made the mistake of playing tetherball with a pro pretending to be a 10-year-old girl and she'd cleaned me. Every time the ball came toward me it was so high off the ground, I couldn't get a fingernail on it. I wouldn't make that mistake again.

It was recess and it was sunny out and that was plenty. A few feet away an older kid was standing with a ball under his arm, also a little at a loss, when a black kid walked up to talk to him. I heard him ask:

"Whatchou doin'?"

"What's it to you?"

"Gotta bet for ya."

"Yeah, what?"

"You'll see. And bring that ball with you."

The black kid motioned with his head and the kid with the ball followed. I tagged along having nothing better to do. The three of us headed behind a backstop. A furious kickball game was being played on the other side. It was a corner of the lowers circumscribed by a chainlink fence and looking out on a sweeping view of the lowerlowers and the View Ridge playfield below that.

There behind the backstop was a slight black kid waiting for his partner. He was wearing a small-brimmed Stetson and looking intensely middle-aged, though he couldn't have been more than twelve.

"This is Ailey," said his friend. "Here's the deal. Ailey is gonna stand where he is and you can stand as close as you want and we'll bet you a quarter you can't hit him with the ball." Ailey stood there stock-still not blinking an eye.

Without a word or a moment's hesitation, the kid with the ball fired away. He had a good arm and almost no windup, just a short, compact recoil and kaboom! From three feet away. The ball crashed into the chain-link fence as Ailey shot backwards about a foot out of the way. The kid scooped the bouncing ball up and fired another volley, this time even faster and harder and Ailey like lightning flew out of the way. Again the ball crashed against the fence. "That's two."

Having begun with little sympathy for the performer, the thrower was determined to give it to him but good, and immediately grabbed up the ball again and whipped it at the ageless dodge ball champ. I couldn't believe that a good thrower could possibly miss someone from pointblank range three times, but there the ball went, nothing but air, smashing into the fence.

"That's three." Irate, the thrower fired again, this time barely grazing the unflappable Ailey. The thrower, visibly impressed, quit trying to break the bones of the thin gentleman before him, and stood smiling with the ball tucked under his arm.

"Gotcha."

"On the fourth try. Seventy-five cents for us for the first three misses, and we give you the last one, though you just barely nicked him. That's minus a quarter which makes you gotta pay us fifty cents."

The kid with the ball uncoiled and fast, hard, and dead on that ball flew by Ailey's ducking head. Airball. Before he could retrieve it Ailey's manager grabbed it.

"Shoulda quit while you were ahead. Now you're down seventy-five cents and I'd pay up if I was you."

"I never bet."

"Whattaya call all those throws, chump?!"

"Practice."

Violence made me sick, probably because I was never sure I wasn't about to become the innocent passerby turned punching bag. I could feel this friendly game of chance about to end in mayhem. "C'mon, pay him," I said. "You took him up on it. What's seventy-five cents."

"It's the principle of the thing," the deadbeat muttered and laughed. Then he shoved his hand into his pocket and pulled out some change, silently counting it. "All I've got is sixty-three cents."

"Give it here."

The poor sport tried to throw it on the ground, but Ailey snatched all six coins dingdingdingdingdingding—out of mid-air. Not really, but I wouldn't have been surprised if he had.

His manager turned to me: "Wanta play?"

"I don't have a ball."

"We can getchou a ball..."

"That's okay. Thanks anyway."

"Hey, any o' you guys wanta try an' hit my friend??" he yelled at the guys on the other side of the backstop who were waiting their turn to kick. "Only a quarter a shot."

I wasn't interested in losing my lunch money to a guy who could dodge a bullet. I'd seen what we were up against. Ailey might have been Johnny Flame, Hermes, Mercury, Speedy Gonzalez, but you couldn't tell right away. Because he kept his wings folded inside his sneakers and tucked inside his hat. He appeared one sunny day behind a backstop on the lowers and I saw him with my own eyes. The World's Fastest Human making some spare change, performing cheap carnival tricks.

Chapter 26.

Some Brain Teasers

Entomology for ten: do mosquitoes bite you because they like you or because they hate you? Entomology for twenty: if you pull two legs off a Daddy Long Legs, does it turn into an insect or a broken umbrella?

I was reading a book and came across a word I didn't know, so I asked Yownskins: "What's 'castration' mean?" "It's when they cut your balls off." Simple question, simple answer.

Etymology for thirty: what's the difference between a faggot of sticks and a pile of fascists? I remember my brother Yownskins letting me see one of the 20th century's grisly photos:

"That's Mussolini," he said, and pointed at a charred corpse strung upside-down like the Hanged Man from a deck of Tarot cards. A crowd was enjoying the sight (along with my brother).

"Who's Moosa Leaney?"

"You don't wanta know." Probably not. "Whistle why you work, Johnny is a jerk, Mussolini bit his wieney, whistle why you work."

Twenty years later, in a cross between snorting and giggling hysterically to himself, my brother announced to no one in particular: "I'm a dwarf. I'm a spastic." Another time he opined: "Maybe I should have been a singer."

Philosophy for forty: Is nostalgia shrinking from life or retreating from death? The first day of school, the first Wednesday in September after Labor Day Weekend was not unlike death. Recess was Life and temporary resurrection.

Kids for fifty: What could be more exciting than knowing you might get caught? Getting caught, then listening humbly, apologizing with due respect, squirming out of the worst charges, weathering the first and second degrees, avoiding the third, with barely-contained, rising euphoria climbing gingerly down off the grill.

Chapter 27.

Full of Bologna

My unswerving fidelity to the bologna sandwich prepared me to be impressed by Coolos' proposal, one day, as we were tip-toeing around his parents' lavishly decorated home that we go down to the kitchen and have "a club sandwich." Mr. Cool's kitchen was an unnerving combination of kitchen and museum. His mother's plate collection was displayed on a thin ledge that ran all the way around the kitchen, twelve inches below the ceiling. As Coolos began the solemn task of making triple-decker sandwiches—turkey, bacon, pickles, cheese, mayonnaise, and lettuce on toast—I kept my attention riveted on the plates, praying to the gods of wretched children. Please don't unleash any earthquakes until we've gotten our food and gotten out of here. In his family, retribution seemed swifter than justice.

The club sandwiches were delicious and unspeakably exotic. My ten-year-old friend frequented restaurants de luxes and then was nice enough to bring their secrets back to a fellow gorged on luncheon meat of unknowable content.

In those days, I was so full of boloney it isn't even

funny. It's all I ever wanted for lunch. "And now the Beardsley Family for Wonder Bread." Still, one day, the no-frills bologna sandwich—Wonder Bread, margarine and lots of mustard—gave way to fine dining: broiled bologna. Two slices of white bread "buttered," laid out on a blackened cookie sheet, a slice of bologna to one side, shoved into the electric oven.

I would broil the bread until it was browned around the edges.

Bologna broiled: a sizzling arc rotated through the material plane, bearing only a greasy resemblance to a parabola rotated around the y-axis, like one of the functions in my brother's trigonometry book. Over time the daily bologna gourmandise was refined, codified. I began to melt cheddar cheese in the hot bowl of bologna—no mustard. Imagine the pleasure throughout my cardiovascular system as I bit into two pieces of toasted white bread drenched in vegetable oil, drenched in cheese and bologna juice, holding a slice of hot bologna the color of red dye #2.

Still I was unaware of the subtle, pungent, oily grasp that the foodstuff had on me. The pureed, pink, and rubbersome habit began to grow wildly from a sandwich a day to two to three. It had me in a headlock and was giving me the Dutch rub. I told myself: "I love bologna."

Some time later I read *The Jungle* by Upton Sinclair. Or heard about it from Yownskins. The rats, the workers' fingers getting mixed right into the sausage. Then my brother made me read the ingredients on a pack of Oscar Meyer "all beef" bologna. Shock therapy. I started eating Space Food Sticks instead.

Winter 1968

Chapter 28.

The Biggest Snowball the World Has Ever Seen

One morning it started to snow and Sallippo made us pull the blinds so we couldn't watch the snowflakes and their mysterious, silent, spinning, drifting descent. Happily it was snowing still at recess. I began catching snowflakes on my mittens to study them. Were they really all different? It was hard to believe. Snowmen rolled to attention left and right, the wet Seattle snow soaking mittens through, hands turning wrinkled and red. Sopping wet, mittens sometimes flew all the way off when kids threw snowballs, breaking the rules. That was getting caught red-handed. After ten minutes of playing in that cold watery snow you could see through the edges of your hands. Every few years it would snow and it would be so cold that the snow wouldn't pack. It was still fun, but not like the sticky stuff that you can make snowballs the size of footballs with. And bounce off the side of heads the size of large melons. Usually a few seconds were devoted to playing a game we could never win: dodging snowflakes, as if it were acid rain or nukular fallout. Or fate. Or time. Though that wasn't what we were thinking about then.

It was like something I heard much later from a sick, elderly, philosophical man, planning the details of his own burial. "You can try to live forever," he said, "but you won't succeed."

In the middle of the mad snow play the freeze bell honked, and I just kept packing a nice big snowball with my bare hands. A girl named Fern spied me and called out: "Knowling's still moving." "Shut up," I hissed, "you fern." I hadn't realized the snowball had her name on it, and I guess it didn't after all. It missed by inches. Linguistics for sixty: How do you conjugate the noun "ferd"? Fern, ferd, inferred, ferdbird, infernoed, fernburgered.

At lunchtime it was still snowing. There was an inch and a half on the ground when we scampered outside and went back to building snowmen, catching snowflakes on our tongues, packing snowballs on the sly. The snow was coming down fast in fat ragged clumps. It wasn't the corny corn snow that would fall sometimes in little pellets and pattered down on the playground in a sort of excited panic. Corn snow just made you wish for real snow—the kind you could pack. This day the temperature was in the high 20's and the snow was plentiful and packable. The blizzard and the sudden appearance of a dozen snowmen made us forget Salerpa and her dark classroom.

On the lowerlowers a clutch of industrious youths were starting to roll a little snowball. Though with each crunching revolution—uhnhh—it grew, adding another and another crust, almost like the rings of a tree. Soon it was a rather big snowball. But it wasn't yet The Biggest Snowball The World Has Ever Seen. From a handful of snow and a common vision it had become a respectable base for a big snowman. The engineers put their shoulders and mittens to the snowball and kept pushing. Leave the building of snowmen to others. Theirs was a grander design. They could have been Egyptian slaves building a pyramid, toiling against insensate matter. But they saw the ice as more than indifferent and uncooperative—it was simply a repository of considerable potential energy. Soon the snowball was as tall as they were and when they put their shoulders to the wheel, it barely tottered in place. It seemed as likely to back over them as advance.

They had drawn a small crowd already, so they incited other junior engineers. Small, eager mittened hands joined the struggle to complete each increasingly difficult revolution. Heave-ho! Heave-ho! The crest of the steep hill down to the playfield wasn't more than twenty feet away. If they were lucky, they would reach it before a playground monitor spotted them. As with any noble cause, people rose up. A dozen boys came running to push them over the top. The originators, who were panting and sweating, stepped back for a moment as their baby, a three hundred pound snowball was shoved to the far edge of the lowerlowers.

"Hold it!"

Everyone stopped pushing. The snowball, which was now six feet in diameter, was perched on the edge of the hill.

"When a car comes, I'll count to three and then we

push like crazy."

The freeze bell rang. No car in sight. The walk bell rang and there was still no car.

"We're gonna be late!"

"Tough titty!"

"No quittin' now. No one leaves before the snowball goes."

"We'll get in big trouble."

"Too late to worry about that now."

"This is gonna be worth it."

"You're not kiddin'."

"Hey, hey, hey, there's a car!"

"Okay, ready?"

"Wait, wait..."

"Okay?"

"Okay!"

"On three. One, two, three!"

A car had come suddenly slowly into view from the south end of 45th street. It was a black Rambler, a car that most people wouldn't give a second glance, a bottom-of-the-line box-mobile.

"You boys know better than that!" a voice boomed from close behind them. It might have been their consciences but wasn't. And it was too late. They'd already started pushing for all they were worth. The snowball lurched forward at first in slow motion, then faster, still growing as it rolled down the hill toward the Rambler.

"I'm gonna tell 'em we were chasin' the snowball, but it was too big and we couldn't stop it," one of the

culprits thought to himself, quickly inventing an inplausible alibi for himself and his cohorts.

"That's Salapa's car..."

It wouldn't have been more terrible to learn that the black Rambler belonged to the prince of darkness. But by then there really was no stopping the snowball and its awesome display of kinetic energy. Water vapor, crystalline and insubstantial had drifted mysteriously down over us, and now, with the help of many hands and human ingenuity, the ephemera was rampaging downhill on a direct collision course with an emissary from the River Styx. And Miss Salyopa, hatching new ways to torment the innocent children under her tutelage, was wholly unaware that The Biggest Snowball The World Has Ever Seen was about to crinkle her faithful box-mobile and drive her mortal remains away to their final parking place.

"Maybe God does exist."

"Maybe we should skip going back to class."

"We'll get twenty years," thought the son of a lawyer.

"What a shot!"

The descent of the snow boulder confounded one of the laws of optics (the vanishing point), and would have created an ideal study in perspective for pre-Renaissance artists. As an object rolls downhill away from a fixed observer, it normally appears to get smaller and smaller. But, a large snowball that gathers snow at the same time is unlike other horrible problems that one day thankfully disappear over the horizon. The already painfully obvious Quite Huge Snowball kept growing, drawing more pointed attention to itself. It was going away and staying forever. Like children, my father might have said.

"Son, whatever you do, don't have children," is how he used to put it, then he'd laugh. One time when taken to task for always offering the same definitive advice, he said: "Well, they're cute when they're small." And then a bit petulantly: "Do you think I would have had five kids, if I didn't like children?!"

My dad used to come home, sit down on the couch with a can of peanuts, and read *The Seattle Times* and *The New York Times* before dinner. About the fifth time I would yell "Dad!" and my Dad wouldn't lower the paper, I would begin to wonder if I'd got the right guy. I'd begin to wonder who the guy behind the paper was, that the name "Dad" didn't mean anything to him. I always wanted to be a writer. Unconsciously, I probably thought I could get my father's attention that way.

Psychologists say that the difference between "mentally disturbed" people and "sane" people is that sane people are able to block out some of the gezillion signals emanating from the body and from the world, are better at compartmentalizing internal and external stimuli into things, people, concepts that are neatly understood. And ignoring the rest. Granted it is taking insensitivity to an extreme, but it is a powerful survival technique for those who would preserve their sanity—tuning out one's family.

As the now titanic snowball steamrolled toward the bottom of the hill, it hit something, a slight bump, a slight ridge, broke in half and like two inverted flying saucers hurtled toward the black Rambler. One half moon skimmed over the hood of the car. The other skimmed over the trunk, but Salappa's infernal luck held. The UFO's test flight was a short one to the principal's office and then back to the drawing board: it failed to put down any landing gear on the far side of 45th and exploded into ten thousand readymade snowballs. The child scientists would have liked to have inspected the smoldering ruins, but they were captured on the spot. What they might have found wasn't uncovered until later—a bent license plate, an antenna, bacteria from space, paint from Sallappa's black period.

Another dangerous educator, Mr. Condorbutt, had seen the launch. "You little...!" his voice boomed out. He was a small man of action with bowlegs and a bristly flattop. He began grabbing what seemed like dozens of spindly arms of the kids who had gotten A Bit Too Rambunctious. The way he might have weeded his garden, if he were in a real hurry, and he began dragging them back toward the building. He didn't say where he was taking them, since he didn't need to.

"Please, don't make me go to jail," thought the lawyer's son.

It must have been gratifying for a small man like Condorbutt to overpower so many ten-year-olds, not to mention some of the great ballistics engineers of the age. He looked like an angry centipede as he retraced the path of the ever-diminishing snowball back to its source, dragging kids by their hair, their ears, their collars, their arms. What worried them was not so

much this flattop or the trip to the principal's office. It was what Sallopa would do.

Moments before, Miss Sallappa just happened to glance in her rearview mirror as a Truly Massive Snowdrift blew past, barely missing the fins of her Rambler. The other half-ton of packed snow blew past the front of the Rambler and tore off her radio antenna.

In her retrospection it was nothing more than a white blur that made a little snap. She twisted around in her seat to try to get a better look at what was going on behind her, but her brassiere cut into her ribs. The top button of her red wool dress choked her windpipe. She gasped. The straw mat covering the hole in the driver's seat scratched her left buttock.

"What's going on here?!" she demanded squirming. "What was that?!" She tried untwisting as she began turning slightly blue in the face. "A white tornado? Got to unbutton!" She tried to work the button free and almost skidded up on the sidewalk. "Watch whoa! The road! My blood pressure! Brake gas turn return sliding slipping! Watch watch. Hey, I see brats! Breaking rules! What are they doing in the park?!"

Sallappa found herself looking out over the flat, white, peaceful expanse of View Ridge Playfield, which was only broken up by chainlink baseball backstops and was colored a deep evergreen by trees lining its western border. "I see you! They'll try to give me some flimsy excuse, but it won't work. I see you Barnes. And who's that other kid? I know. I know." Choking and swerving, she continued to motor implacably back to her classroom.

Moments before, when the snow boulder was still airborne, Mr. Cool and Phil Barnes were loping across the snowed-in park on their way back to school. But seeing the Rambler just excape being totally totaled, Coolos pulled up, staggered two or three steps, threw an arm in the air for effect, groaned, and fell backwards in the snow.

"Don't get up. Sheeit. She's looking this way."

As they watched, the Rambler moved ever more slowly out of view.

"Did she see ya?"

"Probably. You can get up, she's outta sight. Come on. We gotta get back before she does!"

"She turned! She's coming this way!"

They both dove for cover, peering over a snowbank as the malign funereal boxmobile approached along the south side of the playground. It slowed but didn't stop. She was staring in their direction as she passed. Their hearts, their stomachs, their bowels, their jaws—all were falling. The blood was pounding in their ears.

"She must be heading back to 75th."

"Yeah, just wanted to make a little detour to be sure it was us."

"Maybe she'll get stuck and we'll beat her back."

"Come on!"

They jumped up and began raggedly jogging back to school.

"Can you believe it? We almost saw the end of Sawlappa."

"Almost."

"That woulda been cool."

"Yeah, we woulda found her squished inside her car. And we woulda tried to pull her out, but she's so fat it wouldn'ta worked."

"And I'd of looked her right in the eye and said: 'Don't get mad, but the dictionary says that "mad" does too mean "angry." If you still don't believe us, you're crazy!'"

"Please, please, please let Sullappa's car get stuck."

By now they were panting and staggering. They couldn't stop to inspect the shattered snowball. They still had 200 yards and three long, steep staircases to go and Sullappa was en route. Mr. Cool was running in a crouch and Barnes, a big goofy guy who ran with his toes turned out, was loping along, his tongue hanging out. They grunted up the first set of stairs.

"We woulda tried to drag her out of the wreck, but the door woulda been smashed shut and she woulda croaked right there in front of us."

"For a split second there I thought my prayers were being answered."

"Sheesh! That was great! Wait, wait. I gotta rest, just for a sec. I'm gonna have a heart attack otherwise."

Barnes sank down in the snow, took a few deep breaths, and then struggled back up on his splayed, soaking sneakers.

That night Yownskins and I trudged back in the luminous darkness and reenacted a few glorious hours of trench warfare. I wouldn't have thought getting my face washed with snow was one of the more likely perils

of a winter campaign, but my brother assured me it was and he knew more about world war than I did. When I stopped crying he apologized, picked up my wool cap and brushed it off, even patted me on the back. So we decided to fight on the same side and play sniper and pick off enemy stragglers—cars and cats, stop signs, street lamps, and dark empty houses, before we ran for it, huffing and puffing, back across the frozen tundra of the lowerlowers.

Chapter 29.

Yownskins

The body—its intimate parts and intricate functions—the wonders and ridiculousness of it—was a large part of the Things To Know if you wanted to be a real kid in my family. Yownskins was a master. He was like one of the brahmin who masters the beating of his heart. He could wiggle his ears, snear with either corner of his mouth, raise either of his eyebrows independently, turn his eyelids inside-out, make noises with his armpits—squouch, squouch, squouch— distend his stomach so that it looked twice as big as normal, as if he were suffering severe malnutrition. He could turn his naval from an innie to an outie, but only for curiosity's sake. He could recite the alphabet belching. And he could play a dynamite version of "Wipeout" drumming with his forefingers on the kitchen table. He probably should have been a drummer.

He was especially renowned for giving people— strangers—"the eye." He would draw in the lower rim of one eye, causing it to twitch, making him look mean and demented. One Easter, we'd gone camping and were all looking pretty grubby when we found ourselves in the same small town diner with a contingent of local churchgoers in pink and yellow Sunday dresses. When they looked at us with quiet disdain, Yownskins demolished their stares with an extended version of "the eye."

Could I have asked for a better mentor?

Chapter 30.

Who Cut the Cheese?

One evening our Mom asked our sister if she would get up and cut us some cheese. It was a Sunday and we were having our usual Sunday dinner, split pea soup or chili, cheese and crackers. The Onliest gets up, goes into the dark kitchen and gets a block of cheese out of the icebox. She takes down a knife. We hear the clunk of the knife cleaving cheddar and bumping down on the cutting board. She lets out a scream. Uh oh. She's sliced off her arm. I jump up and run into the kitchen. She's screaming and whimpering at a very big, jet black, longhaired horsefly enshrined in a piece of cheese. It looked timeless and dignified as a hieroglyph.

For a split second, I thought my brothers had come up with another good one, but no, this was an impersonal practical joke, like rain on Christmas or getting Sallappa. It wasn't anything personal. The joke was on whomever. For instance, you're propped up in the wrong place (a molded orange plastic chair) at the wrong tick of the clock (3:27:37 p.m.), taking time out (you think) from chewing on a chewburger to remove a piece of gristle stuck between a molar and a wisdom tooth (with your tongue), when the cross-eyed guy with the AK-47 comes in to order some dead meat to go.

Like the time Susie Lynn didn't make it to the nurse's office or to the green metal waste bucket for that matter, but heaved tuna blanquette all over Soolahoop's desk. She apologized and mumbled something about "elementary flu" as she ran for the door. Her doctor thinks she's allergic to grade school, but I bet she's just allergic to Salopa. Freud would have said, it didn't just happen. There was something behind that particular joke. She had her reasons.

Spring 1969

Chapter 31.

Surprisingly Quick for her Age

She stood about five feet tall and was stout as a hog's head. Salappa didn't look like much of a leaper. She was more of a barreller. She was a tank. One hot spring day right before lunch—bang bang bang bang— went a rubber ball against the outside of our brick classroom wall. The class gasped as Salappa scrambled to her feet and barreled out of the classroom. She barged back in seconds later, dragging a little black kid, shoved him in an empty chair. He obviously had no idea what he was getting into playing ball against that wall. He would have had better odds bouncing a ball off the head of a sleeping crocodile.

Chapter 32.

The Gleeful Reenactor

The gleeful reenactor, one of my friends, was known for vivid, hands-on story-telling. He'd launch into the story of a fight he'd seen or heard about and when he'd get to the point where blows began to rain down on some poor unfortunate, he would ask excitedly: "Then guess what he did? Wanna see what he did to him?" And the first couple times, before I knew what to expect, the gleeful raconteur would then slug me or twist my arm, or try to put me in a headlock or a full-nelson. Given a little encouragement, the epic poet would hap'ly have taken a running start and performed a perfectly executed flying kneespike right in the small of my back. All in the name of accurate storytelling. I learned, when given the option, to demur: "No, no, that's okay. Just tell me about it, no need to exert yourself," and I would hold off the sadistic bard with my arms out, trying to take the excitement out of his tale.

Chapter 33.

A Face Like a Pomegranate

From about three feet away, I watched and winced as two kids began fighting in earnest during lunch hour. One was a good-natured, pudgy kid whose giggles rose into peels of laughter and whose excited conversation gurgled along like rain in the gutter. The other kid was a sociopath, the kind of guy who would slam a ball off the back of your head when you weren't looking, to see if you'd take it or give him an excuse to kill you. The good-humored kid had a face like a bulls-eye. His tiny features were crowded into the center of his face like furniture stacked in the middle of a room— the perfect target for the sharp end of a football.

After he recovered from the whiplash and the stars drifted back into the sky, he whirled around to see the sociopath snickering. He squeezed his face even tighter, becoming a twister of righteous indignation, a single point of infinite hatred. Not much of a fighter, he stalked over to the sneering sociopath and thrust out his stubby hands like a crab, opening and snapping them shut, groping for something pinchable. With the butt of his right hand he pushed his enemy's face. He would have smeared the taunting flesh right off if he could have. With his left hand he grabbed his enemy's chest and twisted the baby fat hard as he could. But his enemy bedevilled him with the same face-shoving and fat-twisting. And fists and punches. His face was turning the color of a ripe pomegranate.

The nicer kid always looked out of place in grade school, like a father of four, or a middle-aged insurance salesman. But everyone has his limits, where he reverts back to the primitive scuffling and grappling of animal childhood. Here he was, provoked into pinching and pushing handfuls of baby fat, only to be pinched and pushed and slugged. He was inflicting no more pain than was jolting him and it made him mad! The sociopath gave his face one last vicious twist and his tears dropped like pomegranate seeds. Technically he was the loser, since he was the first one to cry, but he left some fingerprints and after that was left alone.

One of the most brilliant ads of the era: two men in business suits wrestling around on the ground. An anti-war ad that suggested that the heads of nations fight it out themselves if they're so eager to fight. Why are we in Viet Nam?

Chapter 34.

Nam for Dinner

One evening, I was standing in the family kitchen, at the kitchen counter next to my mom, lending a little moral support as she prepared her 15,387th meal, chopping vegetables on the wooden cutting board that pulled out from the counter. She was juggling the nightly meat & potatoes, salad & vegetable menu and I was supposed to be setting the table. But I was watching the evening news. Walter Cronkite had the latest news from Viet Nam and he wanted to share it with the home-viewing audience. We weren't sitting in the living room, though, and we didn't have an E-Z boy lounger.

There's a famous, horrific photo that a still photographer captured on film; but I could swear a t.v. cameraman was also there, to witness the cold-blooded execution of a "suspected Viet Cong" by a Vietnamese sergeant (judge, jury, firing squad).

The suspect was standing there next to his captor, and next to my mom and me, his arms bound. His interrogator lifted his hand holding a gun, and he pointed it at the "suspected Viet Cong's" head, the way the cameraman's camera was pointed at both of them, the way the television was pointed at my mom and me.

But my mom wasn't watching just then, she was preparing yet another nice meal in Seattle.

I watched as the sergeant held his pistol to the suspect's head and pulled the trigger and the suspect

fell right down onto the ground and black & white blood poured out of his head, and the pool of blood pouring out of the side of his head kept growing and spreading. By that age, nine, ten, I'd seen my share of fake killing on t.v., but this was the first real cold-blooded murder I'd ever had to see.

This was not a still photograph of a "suspect" wincing as his executioner coolly blows his life out the far side of his head. This was the moving image of his matter-of-fact elimination. His body flopped on the ground and didn't move at all again, but his blood kept pulsing out in an ever-widening lake of blood, over an ever-widening audience of Americans cooking dinner at home.

My mother happened to look up, maybe I gasped. She tried to shield me from seeing it. She started, panicked, to yell for me to turn the channel, but rushed over to the t.v. herself and spun the dial, and then turned it off. "Gad!" I don't remember what else she said about the war, a murder on the drain board, and our black-and-white t.v. filling with bright red mud and a man's limp emptying body. And in thousands of other kitchens, they heard Walter Cronkite intoning: "And that's the way it is..."

Chapter 35.

Standing the World on its Head

I liked how the world looked when I was standing on my head. I learned how to do it when I was three or four. Later when I had nothing else to do, I would turn the world on its head; it gave me a light feeling, like Atlas at the North Pole.

"Here, let's see if you can stand on your head for the whole time it takes to make two milkshakes. Think you can do it? If you can, one of 'em's for you."

"Okay."

I went to the living room where there was a rug. I nestled my head in the carpet, put my hands down, and took a deep breath. From the kitchen my brother Hade shouted: "Are you up?"

I pushed my feet into the air. "Yeah," I grunted between clenched teeth.

"I'm putting in the ice cream. I'm adding the milk." Then I heard the high-pitched scream of the blender thrown into action and I braced myself for ten long minutes of head standing glory. Two minutes into the ordeal, my brother comes running into the living room to see how I'm holding up. The blender is shrieking away.

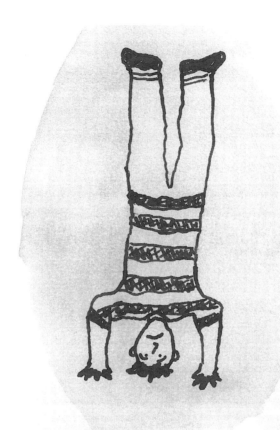

"Can you hang in there? I'm about to add the chocolate sauce." Back he raced to the kitchen and more liquifying. At the five-minute mark, all of the blood in my entire body had drained into my flattening head. My temples were throbbing. My neck, inflamed and quaking, sinews strained to snapping, was telling me to forget it, it wasn't worth it. My eyes felt like they were about to pop. Would *Guinness' World Records*

care? Somebody in India's probably stood on his head for fifteen years already.

"I finished the first one," he yells out. "I'm adding milk to the second one."

My eyesight was going sort of weird on me. Little checks of light and black were shimmering in front of my eyes. My ears were ringing, my feet were falling asleep. I imagined my head attached to the ceiling of a house, plummeting into the abyss.

"Good," I gasped.

It's not that I hadn't put in the time to attempt such a feat. But it was a step into the unknown, like a first marathon.

My brother came running back in.

"I finished the second one, but you can't come down until I pour it and take the first sip."

He disappeared only to come back thirty seconds later with a tall glass of milkshake in one hand and the cooking timer in the other.

"Ten minutes and thirty seconds. Okay, you can come down now."

I rolled out of the headstand and stayed on my back as my blood got reacquainted with my toes. My brother set the milkshake glass by my head.

"For doing such a dumb thing."

I was euphoric, light-headed. "If I become an astronaut, I'm going to be the first person to stand on my head on the moon."

Chapter 36.

Blast Off

NASA seemed to be staging a launch every other week. Salappa would switch on the black-and-white television mounted in the upper corner of the classroom and we would all wait for the countdown. Sometimes the rocket's technical difficulties would make Salapa finally switch off the set and we would have to go back to another social studies lesson with all the optional exercises included.

The countdown was the best part. As the newscaster began "10...9...8..." we would jump in "...7...6...5...4...3...2...1..." and then scream "BLASTOFF!" The flames would start boiling at the base of the rocket, so white they could have been part of the sun, and the smoke poured out the sides of the rocket, more smoke than you'd have ever thought could come out, and for a long moment the rocket would just stay there on the launching pad and I would think, "It's not going to take off!" And then with unnatural slowness, it would rise up off the ground. There never seemed to be any relationship between the sunstream shooting out the base of the rocket and the gradual, lingering ascent of the white space craft.

Then quickly the struggling, leaden missile would become a tiny fireball, jerking in and out of view as the TV cameraman tried to keep up. "It's about five miles up," or "Now it's going about 15,000 miles per hour," the newsman would say, or, "They've just dropped the first stage of the booster," and the rocket would keep getting smaller. And its trajectory would describe an arc that always seemed it might be the beginning of a big mistake, "a terrible tragedy."

One time a couple years before, glued to the TV, we counted down from ten and screamed "blastoff," and the rocket slowly began to rise into the air. Then the capsule just fell off and the three sections of the rocket broke apart, like a puppet whose strings had been dropped. We'd seen enough launches to know that this wasn't the right stuff to see on our black-and-white TV set. We were there to see the latest, greatest American achievement, America winning the space race, America exploring outer space, and there we saw the little snowy image of a rocket cracked in three and astronauts inside burning to death.

Our teacher climbed awkwardly up on a chair and switched off the TV. Did she talk to us about how the best-laid plans can go awry? Or about how complicated a rocket was and how it was asking a lot for nothing ever to go wrong? Or about death? I don't remember. 7...6...5...4...3...2...1. Zero.

Chapter 37.

Inciting a Dirt Bomb Riot

One lunch hour Mr. Cool and I trickled down to the lowerlowers, in pursuit of nothing in particular. It was warm out, springtime, but the ground was still moist. We came bounding down the stairs that led from the lowers to the lowerlowers, slid down the polished metal hand railings, and vaulted off the last of the concrete steps.

We loitered near the northeast wooden backstop, rarely used for baseball, and slowly caught our breath. As I walked in circles, forward, backward, breathing hard, my pal knelt down and examined the moist earth, like a gentleman farmer. Then he reached out and took a few blades of grass between his fingers. Gently he pulled and without murmur of complaint the grass lifted free of the ground, a small but significant lump of moist dirt clinging to it. He rose, straightened his arm behind him, and then as if tossing a hand grenade swung his arm forward. The dirt bomb sailed neatly up and over the backstop.

"Shhhboubgh," he shhhboubghed, watching the happy, light-hearted flight of four blades of grass and a thimbleful of wet sod. Boom shboom.

"Nnnshbonmbgh," the soundeffectsmahn continued, launching another microclod. Its grass tail fluttered through the air. It landed with a soft plop on the other side of the backstop.

I followed the big and small tufts of grass pushing out of the fecund infield mud around to the opposite side of the backstop. There, too, Spring was reaching up out of the mud of the lowerlowers.

Chance always plays the essential intangible part of most euphoric moments. Is the snow just right for sledding or for the perfect snowball—a missile that can be quickly formed, holds together, sails accurately? Is it moist but not so wet that your mittens get waterlogged? Is it not so dry that when you let fly, hoping to deal out swift Retribution, you see the snowball disintegrate yards short of the mark?

Is the ground moist enough to break into hard lumps of mayhem? Will the mud stick to the side of a garage? Or has the mud been cured by a string of warm days, leaving the ground brittle with pounds of dirt bombs for those who know what to look for?

I reached down and pulled gently on a couple tender strands of new grass and found myself holding a perfectly formed dirt bomb. With green streamers. I tossed it over the backstop. "Nnnyarrrr," I sang. "Ynnnngpuh," Coolos rejoined. I was emphasizing the flight, Coolos the explosion, the imaginary cratering of the grade school grounds.

Recreation. Re-creation. The Rec Room. We always thought it was a bit weird that parents called the kids' room in the basement the "wreck room." Gladly! In our more rambunctious moments, the world was a wreck room.

"Nnyyaarrrrr!"

"Krrr."

"Ongggg."

"Whiko, whiko, whiko."

"Bngh, Bngh, Bnnggg."

"Nyanggg."

"Pichhoooo."

"Whiko."

The game became a primitive form of badminton. The dirt birdie would come floating over the backstop and the opposing player would swat the dirt bomb with his open hand. Sometimes it would make it a few feeble feet back into the air. Other times it would fly left, right, back in our faces, over our heads, into the backstop. Floating dirt bombs. Exploding dirt bombs.

The lowerlowers were quite a ways from the main school building, and only the oldest kids, the least likely to wander down to 45th street and get run over, were allowed to play on its grassy, muddy terrain. The playground supervisor didn't devote much time to it, even though it was much larger than the other playgrounds. And so it was that our improvised Spring fun almost went unnoticed as it escalated, new rules and variations appearing as we went along. Other kids wandered down.

In Spring, young boys thoughts turn to chaos and anarchy (i.e., fun). And when presented with absolutely

perfect dirt bomb conditions, they will naturally take up arms. Dozens came and started tossing the miniature grenades so reminiscent of the tiny plastic bombs that James West was using in "The Wild, Wild West" to knock steel doors off their hinges.

Kids fanned out over the grassy knoll sloping down from the lowers to the lowerlowers. Coolos and I were holding the low ground and the stockade. And we found ourselves sucked into the rising conflict. The new arrivals were flinging fist-sized bombs of hard-packed dirt that they were tearing out of the ground and firing at the backstop, each other, and innocent bystanders—girls who had come down to the privacy of the lowerlowers to talk. About boys, I guessed, or the other girls. I never got close enough to know for sure.

Someone threw a dirt bomb with a rock inside and its ringing report exploding against the backstop would have been enough to alert the authorities. But just to leave nothing to chance, a kid threw a dirt bomb up and over the chainlink fence separating the grassy slope from the concrete playground above, clearly having lost his senses. The dirt bomb flew up in a lazy arc and exploded in the middle of swarms of little kids. Dirt shrapnel blew out in a circle from the bomb's epicenter. It was lovely and awe-inspiring but sure to invite reprisals. In the horror and ecstasy of battle, the combatants had forgotten such incidental niceties as the Geneva Convention, international law, the wrath of the God of order and well-wiped bottoms, the principal's office, his rules, his ruler. Sallappa.

We had been idly tossing dirt sprigs over a backstop, playing catch really, when our positions had been overrun by marauding, bloodthirsty barbarians, hellbent on burying our quiet hamlet. We had been frolicking absent-mindedly, innocent as small goats in a field, when a pack of fun-crazed kids began ripping the side of the hill out by the handful.

The grassy slope and the stairs that we had tripped down so freely only minutes before were now riotously alive! One normally quiet, reserved boy who always wore a white shirt and tie to school was throwing his arms around a huge clump of weeds growing next to the staircase and ripping for all he was worth. I stopped in my tracks, staring in disbelief. With determination and adrenaline on his side, the kid managed to tug a twenty-pound shell out of the ground, which he immediately heaved at three other kids, trying to topple them like Jack and Jill. Things do have a way of snowballing. Several other boys followed his lead, tearing huge clumps of tall weeds out of the ground and heaving them down the hill.

"Uh-oh," I thought perceptively. The freeze bell rang and the marauding kids didn't pay the slightest attention. This was a fight for the future of the empire. Egad, man, this was no mere child's play!

"I think I'll slip back to class now," I thought, cringing. I pushed by the dirt bombardiers and hurried, perhaps for the first time, back to an afternoon in Salappa's class. The playground was almost deserted, and so was the hallway. The tardy bell rang as I pushed open Sallappa's door. Mr. Cool had made it back to class first, somehow. He smiled an infinitely slight smile with a dirt smudge on his nose. Sweaty and dusty, I climbed into my desk, hardly daring to look in Salloppa's direction, praying that I wouldn't be tapped by the long middle finger of the law.

The afternoon began like many afternoons. Blinds drawn, oppressive heat, silence, a long exercise to read, Saloppa at her desk correcting papers with vigorous, satisfied, paper-tearing checkmarks. I had trouble reading, just staring at the page of the text, a huge dirt bomb of forboding resting in the pit of my stomach. My mouth was dry as dust. I felt the dread and nausea as on some Judgment Day. Would Saloppa let us have it? Would it be the principal? My parents? Would we get away with it?? Inciting a riot! Mr. Cool's dad might take off his belt.

These weren't outside agitators, it was an inside job. Only kids who knew the lowerlowers intimately and the dirt conditions could have taken advantage of the rain and warming trend. Probably planned the uprising for months to have choreographed it so perfectly. Throw the book at them! "Not the Social Studies book if you please, your Honor. Have mercy." I could see a judge up at his bench wind up and whip a thick legal tome at me. Splat went the flapping book against the firing squad wall. Splat went another. Missed me, missed me, now you gotta kiss me.

My mind kept wandering. Jim and Mimi sittin' in a tree, K - I - S - S - I - N - G. First comes love. Then comes marriage. Then comes a baby in a baby carriage. Gosh, that was fast!

How I started thinking about trees and kissing and babies falling, I don't know. Maybe that was my heart falling through the floor. Or maybe I glanced over at the dark-haired girl I was sick in love with. Maybe for a brief moment her beauty chased away my fear. I began thinking what it would be like to be alone with her high up in a tree on a spring day, a Saturday or Sunday, hidden from view by a maple's big, broad leaves, down at View Ridge Playfield. Other kids might be around running and screaming away, but no one would look up into the tree and we wouldn't be saying anything, just looking at each other. I might reach out and take her hand and the electric shock of her soft skin and her delicate fingers and her unbitten fingernails touching my hand would knock me off my branch.

I would fall backwards but I would try to let go of her hand, because if one of us had to fall out of a big leaf maple, it would be better if it were me. But she wouldn't let go of my hand, she'd try to save me. Then we would both be falling out of the tree and we would miss the thick rough branches, only getting slapped and buffeted by those big light green leaves. I'd fall in a deep fluffy pile of fresh cut grass and she would fall on top of me, and we would check that we were okay and we'd laugh and then she would throw both her arms around my neck and put her head on my shoulder. Spitting grass clippings out of her mouth to speak, she would whisper: "Are you okay? I'm so glad you're okay."

"Knowling! And you! You're wanted in the Principal's office," Salappa said.

"Uhh..."

"Do you know why," demanded Salappa.

"No."

"No."

"You can stop reading. He wants to talk to you about something right now."

Relief whipped across the classroom, a collective sigh from all the kids who weren't summoned.

"I'll go with you to make sure you get there," said Sullappa.

We walked in silence through the deserted halls to the office. The only sound was the tortured creaking of her clothes strained to bursting—zippers grinding their teeth, girdle shrieking, support hose shifting, shoes croaking. I only partially heard the symphony; I was busy choking on the soft-ball sized dirt bomb lodged in my throat.

"These boys are here to see Mr. Doorknob," she announced to the secretaries in the office.

"He'll be right with them," one of them said.

Salapa left and we sat down to wait.

"I feel sick," I whispered.

"You look sick. At least we're missing Salabitch's class," said Coolos. "Think of it that way."

It was the middle of the afternoon. The halls were empty. Everyone was in class. And there we were, special delivered to The Office and The Principal. I sat on the edge of a straight-backed wooden chair, not sure whether I would cry or puke first. It might have lightened up the wait to have The Janitor tossing more sawdust on another vast pool of vomit. Mr. Cool slumped back in his chair, fidgeted around, practically chuckled to himself that I was taking it all so seriously, actually glad that we'd gotten a reprieve from Sullappa.

He leaned over and whispered: "C'mon Vis, it's not gonna be that bad. Just say 'Yes, sir,' and 'No, sir,' and 'I'm really sorry, sir, we won't do it ever again, Mr. Principal, sir.'"

I felt as if I'd been captured and brought before the

enemy chieftain on charges of sabotage, awaiting torture. "He's going to paddle us with that yardstick he has in his coat closet," I thought. "What if they make us take Sellippa again next year!"

"So long as they don't tell my Dad..."

"Boys, this way," said Mr. Doorknob, stepping out of his office.

We sat down in armchairs across from The Principal. He looked at some notes, taking his time before speaking.

"I've talked to a number of your classmates this afternoon about a rock fight that took place on the lowerlowers this noon. They say you took part in it."

Neither of us felt this was the time to chime in with a "Yes, sir," or "No, sir."

"Some say you started it." I couldn't think what to say. Mr. Cool dove in, "That isn't true, sir, it wasn't a rock fight, sir. It was just dirt, sir."

"It was only dirt, sir," I gasped.

"Well, rocks or dirt, we don't allow that sort of activity here."

"No, sir," Coolos said, looking down at his saddle shoes.

"No, sir," I whispered.

"Do you understand that we can't allow that kind of activity to go on?" he asked, looking me in the eye.

"Yes, sir," I said meekly, bowing my head, imitating my friend. I'd never said "sir" before in my life, but this seemed the perfect time to deploy one.

"We'll never do it again, sir," Coolos said eagerly,

sensing that we were about to slip unscathed off the hook.

"Never again, sir."

Would we win an unconditional pardon if we uttered "sir" over ten times before he finished? It actually seemed possible. My stomach began to digest the mud pie.

Doorknob pulled a small notepad out of his desk and picked up a pen. "How do you boys spell your names?" We would have liked to have said something like "I don't remember," or "I dunno," but we spit it out. "What are your phone numbers?" Uh-oh. We gave them. Name, rank, serial number. First I thought we were going to get in Dutch. Then it looked like we were going to get off Scot-free. Now it looked as if we were going to go into the master file, or worse, that we were going to be remanded to the higher authorities.

My parents would probably tell me that they were disappointed in me. That was bad enough. But I felt sorry for Coolos. I saw his Dad haul his brothers upstairs to be whipped with a belt one time for stealing pears. They did some first-rate screaming before he was done with them.

"Okay, you two can go back to class. But if I hear of you doing anything like this again, it's going to be a different story."

"Yes, sir!"

"No, sir! We won't sir!"

We bounded out the door of his office, taking the door directly into the hallway so that we didn't have to pass back by the all-knowing secretaries. Mr. Cool closed the door quietly behind us and then we were running, walking, skipping, and flying all at the same time, grinning like mad.

"He didn't do anything," Coolos was quick to summarize. "I told you, all we had to do was say 'sir' a lot. It was so funny how scared you looked, Vis."

We came roaring around the corner to Sallappa's class and almost ran into Mrs. Oddhorse. We tried to make the impossible switch from insolent and unrepentant to sadder and wiser. Fortunately, we were so close and were going so fast that we were past her before she could object to our lightheartedness. That was my first walk on the moon.

Chapter 38.

Billets Doux

We were down to the last month of the school year, and I still had something important I had to say. I had to tell the dancing dark-haired girl with the missing eyetooth that I loved her. Time was running out. Instead of seeing her everyday at school, summer meant I probably wouldn't see her at all. Maybe she'd move away and I'd never see her again.

Love was turning me into a writer. I couldn't help myself. One day, I took a tiny piece of paper and wrote "I love you." I didn't put my name on it though. That would have been going completely moronic. You never sign a confession, unless you've already been given the third-degree—and been broken.

When everyone headed out of the classroom, I passed by her desk and slipped it quickly under the corner of the Social Studies assignment she'd just started, and then, as if my heart were a helium balloon, I kind of floated out to join everybody at recess.

She didn't say anything later that day. Or even the next. When I looked over at her, she didn't seem to have noticed anything. She looked just the same.

Maybe it got lost, brushed onto the floor, swept up, tossed in the garbage and incinerated.

I had to write her another note. Love was making me do it. I had to. I took a slightly bigger piece of paper, slightly heavier paper, and wrote in slightly bigger lettering "I love you." How was I going to put it where she would find it without anyone seeing me?

When the lunch bell rang, everyone hustled for the door, except the few who had to stay in and go over their corrections with Salappa. I pretended to keep working. Then I slowly went about organizing the things on my desk. Stacking my books. Tidying up my papers. Carefully placing my #2 pencil in the pencil trough. I kept an eye out.

When three or four kids were standing dejectedly at Salappa's desk and she was vigorously etching their work with red check marks, I rose and slid silently down the aisle the dark-haired lass sat in. I was holding the slightly grander declaration of love loosely in my right hand. My nerves were shocking me.

As I passed her desk, I slowed and opened her Social Studies textbook and flipped the note face-up inside the front cover. She's going to see it. She'll find it and she'll know. My heart was beating like a drum. My head felt like a school carnival balloon. I bumped into another desk, glanced toward Sawlapa and the kids around her, no one was watching, so I kept going, and as nonchalantly as possible made a lazy turn around the front of the desks and out the classroom door, like a hydro bouncing around the final turn, gunning it for the finish line.

That was a Friday. The next morning, my Mom was cooking corned beef hash and poached eggs in the kitchen, and I got a call. "Someone wants to talk to you." I was upstairs watching TV. "Who is it?" "A girl." A girl! I rushed over to my parents' bedroom door and locked it. Then I floated over to the phone and answered: "Hello...?" "This is Patty. I'm over at Blarney's, she's here, she wants to say something to you. She wants to ask you something...."

The sun was crashing through the window, the smell of hash and eggs frying was filling the house, and I waited. They were giggling. The sound of the receiver being dropped, picked back up, another voice. "Hi." "Hi." "What are you doing today?" "I'm going to have breakfast in a couple of minutes. What are you two doing?" "Patty slept over and we're..." "Go on! Ask him." "Well, I just called because I wanted to know, are you the one leaving me notes?" (A long pause on my end). "What notes?" "You know, the ones that say 'I love you.'" (Loud giggling in the background). "No." The sound of the phone changing hands again. "We know it's you. So stop doing it. She doesn't like you. And it's not going to make her. So stop bugging her." (More laughing and the line went dead).

"Breakfast's ready!" I slowly went over to the bedroom and unlocked it. Then I trudged downstairs to a warm kitchen, embarrassed, hoping my brothers weren't going to start teasing me about getting a call from a girl, excited to get a call but totally deflated they'd called just to be mean. There was the hubbub of everyone sitting down to a hot breakfast on a sunny day, a strangely good dish, fried corned beef hash with its weird bits of stuff all smushed together. And my Mom asked: "Who was that?"

"A couple of girls from school wondering about Social Studies."

Chapter 39.

It Only Got Worse

Once I wrote "I love you," it only got worse.

I couldn't concentrate at all that week. By Friday, I couldn't wait to bolt out of there. I couldn't stand another second. Blarney's friend, Patty, kept making faces at me and sticking her tongue out. Blarney, who was shy, ignored me. One time I passed the two together going out the door of the classroom and they made a point of going off into peels of laughter.

Friday afternoon, I got my Social Studies homework back. I'd missed half the questions and had even forgotten to do a bunch of required optional exercises. My paper was so covered with red slashes, it looked the way I felt—smarting from a thousand paper cuts. At the top were written three little words no one ever wanted to read in Salappa's perfect cursive writing: "Please see me."

"Knowling! Come here and bring your Social Studies assignment."

She waved me over. I went up to her desk, trying not to get too close. Her textbook was open and I could see all the answers printed in tiny red lettering. What I wouldn't do for the teacher's copy of the textbooks. "If she's so smart, why does she need to be told the answers?"

"You're slipping, Knowling."

What to say to that? What could I say? "I'm not slipping. I'm dying." I didn't say anything.

"You're going to have to stay in during afternoon recess and redo this assignment. You didn't do the last five sets of optional exercises! I want to see all of them before you leave school tonight."

"But...."

"No ifs, ands, or buts about it! Go write your name on the blackboard!"

I went and wrote Knowling in the one tiny space not crowded with names.

The bell for recess rang and I started to jump up, when I remembered. Social Studies. Optional exercises. The only thing was to try to do them as fast as I could, so I wouldn't have to stay after school, too. What was I supposed to be learning about? Oh yeah, crop rotation in Iowa. What are the optional exercises on? Oh yeah, the importance of letting fields lie fallow. Appropriate enough. That's what the whole year's felt like.

I began skimming the chapter, picking out the answers, dotting my i's and crossing my t's.

Then Salappa did something she'd never done

before. She got up and said: "I'll be right back." Then she waddled out of the room and shut the door behind her. I had a couple seconds to myself. I felt a flush and a rush of mad abandon.

I tore a piece of paper out of my notebook. It was even bigger than the last, maybe two inches by four inches. And then, as if in a trance, I made my hand write "I love you" in letters that I found alarmingly large, alarmingly legible. Should I put an exclamation point at the end? Yes! Love was making me into an exclaimer. No matter what she said, I was going to keep writing her.

Now quick. Before the witch gets back. Quick, quick. I popped up and zipped over to the cloakroom, where all the kids' coats were hanging on hooks. It had rained a little that morning and everyone had come to school in raincoats. But the sun had broken through, and kids had left their coats behind and were playing outside. Faintly I could hear shouts and balls bouncing.

There was her yellow raincoat. It was made of the thick kind of plastic, yellow and shiny, with pockets but no hood. I slipped my hand into her pocket. It was empty. I took the note and read it one more time, then I plunged ahead and slid the note in her pocket. It was desperate, abject. The same simple note. Three little words. A naked declaration of love. I hadn't changed. My feelings were louder than ever. My heart was thumping like a kickball.

As I was scooting back to my desk, light-headed, aglow, rushing like a zeppelin, the Hindenberg, I thought with satisfaction: "She's going to put her hand in her pocket on the way home, maybe just a few feet outside of school, and she's going to find out that I still love her. In capital letters. Tough if she doesn't like it."

The door opened with a whoosh as I was about to take my seat. I looked back to see Salappa eyeing me. "Oh, I had to sharpen my pencil is all," quickly holding up my hand as if I were holding a pencil. I eased back into my chair and tried to remember where I'd been, before the secret of love had carried me away. "Alfalfa, alfalfa, alfalfa... soybeans...." Thanks to Salappa's insistence, my writing was extremely legible.

In an hour, if Blarney remembered her coat, she'd find my note and read "I love you!" With the shred of attention I could muster, I wrote: 8. Corn. 9. Wheat. 10. Sorghum. 11. Loco weed.

Chapter 40.

Another False Alarm: A Sack of Mud

That afternoon, I came rolling down the alley after school and when I got to the west side of the house where the garage was, the Artist and his friend Loogey were crouching up on the roof, about eight feet off the ground, looking down at the driveway. Loogey had a fairly big bag of mud in his hands.

I skidded to a halt.

My brother nodded at Loogey and he starts into a long yell of a scream, the last shrill despairing cry of someone falling, with no chance of surviving, definitely dying. Then his friend heaved the bag of mud and it exploded with a kind of disappointing "flap" flop on the driveway.

"Cut," said the Artist, after a few seconds, and I saw that he was holding a mike and our reel-to-reel tape recorder was next to him, slowly turning.

He rewound and played it: "Aiiiiiiiiiiiiiiiiiii-...plawphshhplttttt." They snickered to themselves.

The next day, they had one of their friends lie in front of Roosevelt High School in his socks, and on the second floor, in Mel Derango's study hall, situated directly overhead, they had someone lean out the window holding only a pair of shoes. When Derango walked into class, they replayed the scream.

That year, Mel Derango fell for another practical joke every day for a month. At the beginning of the year, when everyone in study hall filled out a class card with his or her name, someone filled out one for a guy named "Lem Ognared." Every day Derango would call Ognared's name, and towards the end of the self-perpetuating joke's natural life, he began asking petulantly: "Has anyone seen Ognared? Is he skipping? Does anyone know Ognared?" Even he didn't know Ognared, and he should have.

In our neighborhood, Loogey's older brother was a well-respected poet laureate. He didn't say anything for the first three years of his life, not a word, then one morning his mother made the mistake of toasting him a piece of raison bread.

"What the hell is this?" he asked. As my mother liked to say: "He just never found anything worth commenting on before that."

Chapter 41.

Last Day of the School Year

The last few days each school year were anticlimactic. End-of-year tests were over, but we still had to come an extra day or two or three. Our spirits had split when we handed in our last tests, but our bodies still had to grind out the time.

This year of all years drew to a dull and desperate close, and we talked a lot about what we could do to get back at Sullappa. "The last day of the year, I'm gonna open the door to Salappa's class and I'm gonna yell: 'Mad doesn't just mean crazy! It means angry too!' And then I'm gonna slam the door as hard as I can and run. My Stingray's gonna be right outside for my escape."

"If she chases you, give her the finger."

"If I didn't have to come back next year, I would."

"Why don't we just open the classroom door and when she looks up we can hit her with about ten eggs. I'd love to see her duck behind her desk and us still pelting her with eggs."

"She's such a witch."

We didn't do any of that stuff. We wouldn't have lived out the day. Instead, when it finally was 3:10 p.m.

and the bell rang, we danced out of class and out of fifth grade. Kids were yelling and whooping and shouting and laughing and cheering. Everyone slammed their lockers as hard as they could, books and papers tumbled across the hall. And we kicked the double doors open to get on outta there. Is there a better feeling than the end of the last day of school?

Chapter 42.

Why So Volcanic?

What made Salappa such a hard-ass? Did she hate the world because it hated her? Or did the world hate her because she hated it. Which came first, her hatefulness or her being hated? Did someone mistreat her as a kid? Break her heart as a young woman? Humiliate her as an adult? She was like a volcano or an earthquake. A force of nature. A legend in her own time.

Did she have a two-headed son from some hasty, awkward act of fertilization in the back of her black Rambler? Was he locked away in her basement, in pitch darkness, chained to the wall?

Did red ink clog her veins? Was she correcting kids' papers in blood? Was she evil or just unhappy and lonely? Was she the devil's mother-in-law or just cranky? What a difference it would have made if instead of teaching grade school she'd opened a Skeeball parlor.

Salappa was a stickler. She was a stickler for all kinds of fine points of education. One she made a big deal of was that we should pronounce "wh" as if we were blowing out a candle. The more exaggerated the whistling sound you made, the happier she was. Coolos and I would amuse ourselves by saying "hhhhwhhhhat! did you say?! hhhhhhwhhhhere! do you think you're going?! hhhhwhennnn! am I going to get your corrections on optional exercises D, E, F, G, H, I, and J?!!" That kind of thing.

She was a stickler, like a barnacle. She was a stickler like hot pizza sauce on the roof of your mouth. She was a stickler like burnt eggs on a frying pan. She was a stickler and I was slipping. We were naturally incompatible.

Chapter 43.

Burning Notebooks

When I got close to home, I saw smoke coming from our backyard. I saw fire! Yownskins and his friends were sitting around a bonfire, cheerfully feeding loose-leaf paper into it. Their high school three-ring binders were sprung, and they were liquidating their homework a few assignments at a time—French, U.S. History, Geometry, Trig, English, Social Studies, Chem, Physics—glancing at them with distaste, chucking them into the fire. When they'd torched a year's worth of homework, they threw their binders in, too. Nihilists. School wasn't over for one dumb friend of theirs, though, who tried to retrieve his notebook too soon after the flames died down and burned the crap out of his hand.

"Year after next, I'm going to junior high school. And I'm gonna have a notebook and a bunch of different classes," I thought. "And when the year ends, I'm gonna know what to do. I'm gonna have a bonfire and burn all these boring assignments, Assbite through Fucwad. And especially the optional exercises! June rain better not come 'til all this paper's all burned to hell."

Years later, I asked my brother about Salappa, and he said: "She liked me. Gave me pretty good grades. Salappa. She was pretty good. Pretty good." And that was my introduction to revisionist history.

Summer 1969

Chapter 44.

I Had a Dream: Black & White & Red All Over

The first week of summer, I was alone watching my parents' black-and-white television. It was a quiet, warm day. A commercial came on and it was in color!

What company was it? I don't remember. They announced: "Soon all black-and-white televisions will be able to transmit color programming just like this. We have developed a revolutionary new technology and will be bringing it soon to your home."

Finally, real progress! As the commercial ended, I jumped up and ran to the head of the stairs and started yelling to anyone who might be around. Everyone wondered what I was hollering about. I explained to my Mom and siblings what I'd seen. But I was the only one who'd caught the show. No one else had seen it. And I never saw another one like it. The Greatest Technological Breakthrough in History. Hushed up and buried.

Chapter 45.

Parachuting

One warm June morning, I was staring out the window at Lake Washington. Some people were parachuting and I just happened to look out as they were drifting down through the still, silent, balmy day. As I watched, one of the jumpers looked as if he'd landed in the lake. Then another landed in the drink. I ran and grabbed a pair of binoculars and tried to see what was happening out there over a mile away. They had definitely landed in the lake, but I couldn't see clearly if they were in trouble or maybe just wet. They could be in trouble, but they were so far away, and voices don't carry that far, and I couldn't see any movements from where I was, however panic-stricken. I knew they had missed the ground, the Sand Point Naval Base. Was this just part of their military training? Were they hopelessly tangled in their chutes, right then, as I watched from too far away to do anything to help? Was I watching their death struggle? All was muffled in stillness.

The Seattle Times came that afternoon, an indifferent messenger, and there on the front page was the news that two parachutists had drowned after accidentally falling in Lake Washington. While it happened the world seemed so peaceful, so different from the story about two people "drowned" and the enlarged photo of the two parachutists in black-and-white dots. So different from what the two went through. I had seen, but hadn't been sure of what I was seeing, and now I knew what I'd seen, except I'd been so far removed from someone tangled in the cords of a parachute, the folds of wet material, gasping for air, thinking final frantic thoughts, saying goodbye to dreams, friends, family. A distant spectator to two lives brought to nothing. My mother's first husband, an

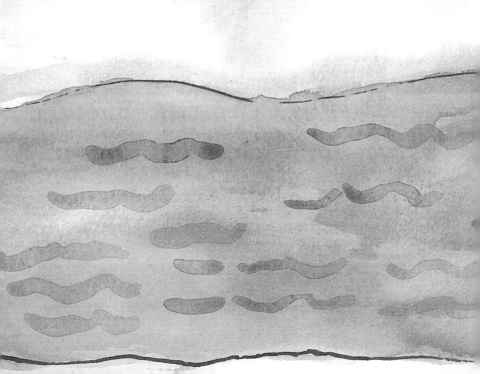

American pilot in WWII, passed his last moments fighting like them alone with the ocean. They don't know where he went down, though any grave is as wide and deep and unfathomable as the ocean, or a life. For the parachutists, it was a patch of water thirty feet deep, a hundred yards from the western shore of Lake Washington—their parachutes winding sheets—glimpsed from afar as still as water lilies on the surface of the lake.

Chapter 46.

Madness

After an entire year, I still didn't know how to spell Salappa. But we found her address in the phone book—4910 Evanston Avenue North. She lived just south of the Woodland Park Zoo.

"Mom, could you give us a ride? We're thinking about going to the zoo."

"That's a wonderful idea. Let me just finish up a few things I have to do and then I'd be glad to give you a ride."

It had been as simple as that. Minutes later, we climbed out of my mom's Malibu and headed to the zoo entrance. But we didn't go in. We just waited until my mom drove off.

"Let's synchronize our watches."

I looked down at my Batman watch. "I've got 11:02."

Mr. Cool looked at his Spiro Agnew watch. "I've got 10:59. Let's set 'em for 11:00." "Okay." It was essential in this kind of operation to synchronize watches. We'd seen it dozens of times on TV... Mission Impossible... I, Spy.

"Let's case the joint," said Coolos, sounding as if he knew what he was talking about.

"We don't have to do anything, do we? We can just kind of look, right?" I said, getting cold feet.

"This is gonna be great."

We turned our backs on the zoo and walked to 50th Street. "Don't stop. Don't look. And don't listen." There was a gap in the traffic and we darted across the busy street and began walking down Evanston, walking on pins and needles, looking for Salappa's house. As we looked south, we could see the top of the Space Needle. Which meant that from the top of the Space Needle, if there'd ever been a clear day, you could have seen Salappa.

We didn't have to walk far. Two houses in, on the east side of the street, was a big, yellow duplex that looked like a barn. The doorway closer to 50th and the zoo was 4910. We'd approached from across the street, so we scrunched ourselves down in the weeds behind a telephone pole and peered over at the house.

It was strange how unexceptional it was. Just a two-story boxy house with three concrete steps up to the front door and a few small windows. To the north, on the corner of 50th and Evanston was a brick apartment building. Its parking lot ran along the side of Saloppa's house, a chainlink fence separating them. From the parking lot, we could see around in back. From the front it looked lifeless, Salopaless. Megalopolis. No black Rambler parked out front.

"What if she has little kids locked in her basement? You know, like teacher's pets?"

"I'm gettin' the hell outta there."

"Not as fast as me."

"Where's the Rambler?"

"It's gone."

"Maybe it's getting repaired and she's home."

"We'll just run."

"Are you sure we should do it?"

"Definitely, Vis."

"Sheesh."

"I'll be right back."

Mr. Cool ran into the building's parking lot, hugging the apartment. At the far end of the lot, he crept over to the fence and looked into Salappa's backyard. There was a garage in back. The door was up and it was empty. The concrete backyard was level with the basement. No grass, no garden, no trees.

Half walking, half running, he recrossed the street.

"I'm gonna get a closer look."

"Be careful."

He chuckled. "Here goes nothin'!"

Coolos had the courage of ten Knowlings. His basic attitude was one of not giving a rip. He scurried straight toward Salappa's house, looking left and right, left and right, hunkered over the way he always ran. He trotted along the north side of the house, pushed open a small fence, and jumped down into the backyard. I felt as if scores of grasshoppers were trying to get out of my stomach. I wanted to run away, like mad. I could feel my feet practically running without me.

A bee came over to see what I was doing lying in the grass. When it droned into my ear I jumped up and started flailing around. It was too late to chicken out. Coolos had reappeared around the corner of the house and slowly extended his forefinger. It was a sign, the coast was clear.

I bolted across the street. My heart was beating so hard I could barely breathe. Was I dreaming? A dead bush along the side of the house scratched my face and I knew I wasn't. We were about to drop down on the concrete driveway behind the house when we heard a car coming. We squeezed into the dead bushes and held our breath. A red station wagon eased past.

Even in my panic-stricken state, I noticed that one of my friend's saddle shoes was untied and that he was standing on the lace. My parents had drilled fear into me, that a potential danger was an inevitable outcome. Bars of soap in the bath, banana peels underfoot, untied shoelaces: all were absolute causes, leading inexorably from A to B—your downfall. You would slip and fall and split your head open. As my mind reeled with fatal slapstick, he started forward, tripped exactly as I had feared he would but caught himself with two lunging steps into a hydrangea.

"Sheesh."

"Let's get outta here."

"C'mon, Vis. Mad does too mean angry. And, gosh-o-lee, am I mad."

Coolos hopped down and his shoes slapped the concrete. I cringed but followed anyway. We ducked into the open garage and listened. Silence. My friend went over to the door to the house. He tried turning the doorknob. It was unlocked. He turned the doorknob, gave it a little push, and it swung open. He listened for a few seconds then crept inside. I took one more look out the garage toward the street, saw nothing and followed, closing the door behind us. We were in a dark, stuffy hallway with two closed doors and a stairway. From the foot of the stairs we could see another closed door at the top. Mr. Cool pointed as if to say, "I'm going up." He slowly painfully climbed the carpeted stairs. After listening with his ear pressed against the door, he turned the doorknob and silently pushed it open. On the far wall of a cramped kitchen he saw a Seattle Public School calendar.

He waved me on up. I climbed the stairs to where I could see the red-white-and-blue calendar. It really was Sullappa's house. The blue days were school days. The red days were weekends, holidays, and summer vacation. The red days of anarchy. The blue days of assignments and the blues. If they'd designed the blue days with red stripes for recess and lunch hour, it would have been less depressing.

The worst months, you can ask anyone, were the months where every week had five blue days and only two red days. October, January, March, April, and May. September started late. November there was Thanksgiving, December Christmas, February Lincoln's Birthday and Washington's Birthday, June the school year was finally, finally over. Summer vacation began three months of red letter days.

Salappa had written here and there on the calendar

in her perfect cursive handwriting. Today's date had one note: "Bingo." The house was dead silent.

From the kitchen Mr. Cool and I stepped into a tidy, sunny livingroom. In front of an overstuffed armchair was a folding tray that she must have eaten off. A heavy black-and-white TV stood against the opposite wall.

"Vis, c'mere quick!"

I followed the sound of his voice around the corner and down a hall. There he was, holding onto the muzzle of a small black dog with both hands, shaking it like crazy. They struggled silently, weirdly. The mute mutt wasn't putting up much of a fight. Mr. Cool laughed and let it go. It was dead. Stuffed.

"Holy moly! His name tag says Illinois!"

"That's not his name. That's the state." A lap dog with an Illinois dog license around its neck. "There is no noise in Illinois," he chuckled. "Have you looked down there?" I asked, pointing to the far end of the hall. "Uh-uh," and he was off again, quietly opening doors one after another. A closet. A bathroom. Her bedroom.

The heavy curtains in the bedroom kept most of the sunlight out, but we could see on her night table a stack of fat romance novels. On a bookshelf, she had *The Collected Essays of Benito Mussolini, Our Friend the Reindeer, The Last Hours of Savonarola, The Autobiography of Vasco da Gama,* and an *Unabridged Webster's Dictionary.*

"All right!"

"This thing's a muthuh!"

It took both of us to lift the unabridged dictionary onto her night table. Then we each pulled out a red pen. Mr. Cool had a red Lindy ballpoint and I had a red indelible Marks-a-lot Marker. Then we sort of poured the dictionary open. I began flipping madly past anger and envy, greed, gluttony, lust, pride, sloth, then back again, back and forth until I found a string of meanings for the word "mad." The ninth definition was "Affected by rabies; rabid."

It was the fourth definition we were looking for: "Informal. Angry, resentful." There it was in the dictionary: "mad" means "angry." I uncapped the fine-point Lindy and drew a neat circle around that definition twice. Then taking the Marks-a-lot, Mr. Cool drew a fat circle around the entire list of definitions for the word "mad." We closed the dictionary and lugged it back onto the bookshelf.

For a second we forgot ourselves. We were euphoric, ridiculously self-satisfied, savoring our simple revenge—correcting the corrector. In red ink. Outside her classroom, higher authorities agreed with us.

Suddenly, we heard the sound of a simple, almost extinct American car, box-like in structure, funereal in color, pulling into the garage. The funeral cortege had come to call. We heard the sharp shriek of the hand brake being yanked home.

"C'mon!" I yelped, and started running. Coolos didn't need any encouragement. We scampered out into the hall, running toward the kitchen, the back door, and, maybe, if we were lucky, another hour of

Life. As we pushed open the swinging door to the kitchen, we saw Miss Salappa already there at the back door. Her glasses and the frazzle of her frizzy red hair were all that could be seen in the window.

"Go back, go back, the basement!" We streaked down the basement stairs, shutting the door behind us as quietly and quickly as possible. From the basement's cool darkness we could hear Salappa's shoes tapping a funeral march. Apparently she was coming home from the grocery store, because we could hear her putting down heavy sacks on the kitchen counters. Canned food clacked against the tile counter, and we heard the fridge open and close several times.

As we were tugging away, struggling to open a basement window, we heard the sound of ice cubes falling into a glass. Salappa's overstuffed shoes shuffled out of the kitchen and squeaked across the living-room. She turned on the TV and we heard her say "Oof!" as she eased into her overstuffed chair. Maybe it was the chair that said "Oof!" She was looking forward to lunch and a little overstuffing herself.

"It's painted shut!" I whispered. "Aren't there any other windows?" We began looking in every corner, dark, dank, dusty. Suddenly we heard her jump up. The chair bumped and groaned, and we heard her marching double-time in the direction of her bedroom. Or was she coming for us in the basement?

"We left the light on in her bedroom..."

"We're fuccing dead!"

"Mommy!"

"Gotta find some way out."

"The backdoor!"

"Upstairs?! I'm not goin' back up there!"

Mr. Cool noticed a door with a latch on it. He cautiously pulled on it and it swung open. What lay inside looked as if it had been forgotten for decades. The space had a dirt floor, and there was some canned stuff and some jars of other stuff, all probably petrified, and there was a cot with moldy blankets on it.

Was it a bomb shelter? No, there was a leash. A leash wrapped around something slumped against the wall the size of a really big dog or a really lanky teenager. A murdered lover? A two-headed kid? Some poor animal snatched from the Woodland Park Zoo? A dusty leash in a forgotten dungeon. Our hair bristled, shrieking with electricity, adrenaline.

Above the hollow thing, whatever it was, and behind what looked like a yard of cobwebs, was a small, dirt encrusted window!

"Close the door! Lock it!" I fumbled to do it, dreading the dark closing us in with the dead, but dreading it less than the living Salopa upstairs, storming around hunting for us.

If we stood on the thing slumped against the wall, we could probably just reach the window latch. But neither of us wanted to go near the thing slumped against the wall.

Both of us noticed something else about the dark space.

"It smells like crap in here!" The floor wasn't really

made of dirt. Mr. Cool hunched over his saddle shoes and crept over to the dead thing on the leash. It had huge furry antlers. The spiders had known what to do with them.

"Rudolph!"

We were both paralyzed until we heard the basement door slam shut and heavy footsteps come hammering down the stairs. Coolos grabbed onto the horns and began climbing the dead reindeer. I braced him as he climbed up and up until he could reach the window and wrench on the window latch with the superhuman strength of Mr. Cool. It budged, just a bit.

He wiped some of the dirt away and could see the outside through the window. If we could get it open, freedom! He tore at the window latch again and this time it gave way. Now all he had to do was swing the window in. When he yanked on it, it scraped open with a dull creak! The footsteps hammering in the basement stopped.

Mr. Cool squirmed headfirst through the window as I stood on the reindeer's back and shoved him up from below. His saddle shoes scraped the bottom of the window as he dove out of the basement. I wondered for a second how I was going to get out. Then I started climbing the antlers like some sort of mad mountain goat. As I grabbed onto the window ledge, my foot slipped off its horny foothold, leaving me dangling, legs flailing.

Just then Coolos shoved the window open again, barely missing my head, and grabbed onto my wrists, braced his feet against the side of the house, and began pulling for all he was worth, grimacing and grunting. I started slipping, sliding up and out, as if Sullappa's house was giving birth to a ten-year-old.

I didn't even have time to get up off the ground before the back door banged open and Salappa came flying out.

"Stop, you!" she snarled. Fortunately, unfortunately (depending on your point of view) she was in such a rush that she skidded on her welcome mat and then, as if she were sliding into second base, she slipped feet first off her back porch and crashed, sliding slowly down to the ground, one step at a time, until she slumped, humped in a heap at the bottom.

"Jesus, that's the scariest thing I've ever seen..."

"Salappa dying?"

"Smiling!"

"Omigod!"

"Did you pay attention when we learned mouth-to-mouth resuscitation?"

"No way!"

"Me, neither..."

"I remember, sorta, but forget it."

We inched over to Sullapa. She was still breathing, which was definitely a good sign. Her eyelids began twitching. She opened an eye.

"Help me, boys..." she murmured.

"Want us to call an ambulance?" I asked.

"Please... I can't move an inch."

Here was the moment we had waited for for so long. Mr. Cool piped up: "Look, Sullappa, we'll call a doctor if you admit that you always knew really that 'mad' also can mean 'angry.'"

"Didn't."

"Your own dictionary says so."

"Informal usage, colloquial expression. Doesn't count."

"Then there's not much we can do. If you won't budge, neither will we."

"You little j.d.'s are making me mad!"

"See! You said it yourself."

"But I meant 'crazy.' You'll be sorry you've made me mad!" She struggled until her face turned the color of a pomegranate. Still she wasn't able to heft herself up off the ground. Then she passed out again, and the same weird smile spread across her face.

"We can't leave her like this. I hate her, but I don't want to kill her. Not completely."

"We didn't kill her. She slipped on her own."

"I'm gonna call 911."

"Don't give 'em your name! Tell 'em you're a concerned citizen."

I stepped back a bit, got a running start, leapt over the prostrate Salappa, and ran back up the stairs and into the house. I dialed 911 and informed them that an old woman, hideous in demeanor, was lying on her back at the foot of some stairs, unconscious. They promised to come right over.

Then I just sat in a chair in the kitchen for a moment and stared at her school calendar, and the date, August 2, 1969, and I couldn't help noticing that in spite of everything, it was sort of a red-letter day. And I realized that if we got put in prison for real, there wouldn't be even two red days in seven.

I drifted back outside, got a running start and jumped back over Salappa. Coolos was sitting cross-legged about five feet away from her.

"We need a good title for this one."

"Peanutbuttuhmahn Strikes Again?"

"Rambunctious."

"Bambi Meets Godzilla."

"The Cave of the Gross Christmas Ornaments."

"...and Buttwax."

"The Wild, Wild Northeast."

"Talk later..."

"Think she'll need a head transplant?"

"We'll tell 'em we're conscientious objectors. We couldn't let Sullappa warp any more kids."

"Telling them mad doesn't mean angry."

"Miss Salappa, are you awake?"

"You're a couple of little hoodlums," she groaned.

"Sheesh. We called 911."

"All the optional exercises. No recess. Lunch in the classroom. With me," she threatened, getting her strength back.

"She lives, we're doomed. She doesn't, we're fucced."

Before she could haul herself off the ground and start wringing our necks, the medics came around the side of the house.

"She slipped on her back steps," we explained partially. "Looked like maybe she was getting a little too rambunctious, in a little too much of a hurry. You slipped, isn't that right, Miss Salappa?"

Salappa didn't say anything. Instead she strained to lift her head to get a good look at us. We kept moving around behind her, trying to stay out of line of the evil eye. It took four husky paramedics busting a gut to lift her onto a stretcher, as if they were trying to balance a watermelon on a butter knife. Lucky for us, she was a lot tougher than a watermelon. Otherwise, all the medics could have done when they got there was help us pick up the red pulp and the cracked rind. And they wouldn't have helped us spit out the seeds either.

Of course, the police also came by to visit. As the medics carried Sallapa to the ambulance, we were warned to stay put, that we had some explaining to do. I felt too weak to want to make a break for it. Mr. Cool thought if we really hurried, we could still make the Canadian border.

"They're gonna kill us!"

"Nah, Walla Walla, at the very worst. We're only ten. They're not gonna kill us."

"Our parents I'm talkin' about."

"Oh yeah, them, maybe."

"What if they made us take Salappa all over again next year?"

"All we did was draw two circles in her dictionary."

"Yeah, but, before that, there was the breaking and entering."

"Yeah, right."

The thing about the word 'mad' was not that she wasn't sort of right, that 'mad' can mean 'crazy.' It's just that that's not the only answer. A lot of the time, mad means angry. And then sometimes when people get angry, they also go mad.

People who are partially right but who want to be totally right are crazy. Here all we do is point out to Sollapapapa that she's not completely right about something that she'd been making a big deal about, and she has a cow.

"If she hadn't slipped, she would have..."

"...killed us..."

"It's too bad she got so mad that she did that flying knee-spike..."

That's the problem with revenge. Your plan may seem simple, poetic, reasonable—righteousness clearly on your side—next thing you know you're ankle deep in reindeer crap, scrambling to escape the gallows.

Chapter 47.

Bruiser

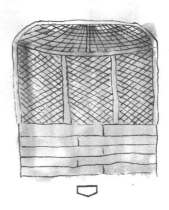

The Seattle Pilots brought Major League Baseball to town that year. The Pilots traded some rookie named Lou Piniella before the season got underway. Tommy Harper stole 73 bases that season. Jim Bouton wrote *Ball Four* about the fun of playing in Sick's Stadium for our expansion team. It was great having a big league ball team. Too bad they sold them after that one year to Milwaukee where they became Brewers.

They held the Little League baseball tryouts at View Ridge playfield one Saturday morning in the spring. As I was waiting to take my turn fielding a grounder, I looked up toward the lowerlowers and saw the dark-haired girl and some friend dancing along the top of the hill in the sunshine. "She must live close to the playfield!" When it was my turn to show how I could use a glove, distracted, I muffed a grounder, letting it dribble right through my legs, then, when one of the other kids handed the ball back to me, I made up for it by wildly overthrowing the kid playing first base. The ball smashed ridiculously high and wide on the chain-link fence.

Some people have said that the appeal of baseball is numeric, the numbers, the stats. For me it was the heroes and the lingo. The Big Train. Walter Johnson. Satchel Paige. Sandy Koufax. The Babe. Ty Cobb. Honus Wagner. Henry Aaron. Brooks Robinson. Frank Robinson. Boog Powell. Willie Stargell. Manny Sanguillen. Rod Carew. Bob Gibson. Lou Brock. Tommy Harper. Leon Wagner. Big Daddy Wags.

A Texas Leaguer was a bloop single. Not much you can do about that. The luck of the batter. Picked off. Planting yourself on the front edge of the dusty pitching mound and throwing strikes. Pitching from the stretch, holding the runner on third. The screwball. Carl Hubbell threw screwballs, and he ended up walking around with a left arm that bent so far around, it looked as if he'd been born with two right arms. I was a lefty, holding the ball's seams parallel to my fingers and throwing screwballs without half trying.

If you're a lefty, you always throw curves at lefties. Southpaw. Giving up back-to-back homeruns. The shame of the backward K, whiffing without taking the bat off your shoulder. Playing catch with the catcher. Looking for the sign. A pitchout. A strike at the knees. A clutch base hit. The error that turned things around. They were calling for rain later this evening, but here it is.

The suicide squeeze play, where the player on third

breaks for home as the pitcher is making his pitch, and hopes his teammate manages to lay down a decent bunt. Hopes he doesn't decide to swing for the fences. Stealing home. Taking a big lead. Laying one down. Turning the doubleplay. Double Bubble. Spitting. Infield dust in your mouth, you have to spit. Getting a strawberry on your hip sliding into second. A hard slider. A hot box. Bases loaded, 3 and 2. Batting .300. Batting .400. A headhunter. Beaned him. The spitball. Doctoring the ball. The drag bunt. Inside at the belt. An infield pop-up. Bailing out on an inside pitch.

That summer, I ended up on a little league baseball team with a pitcher named Bruiser. It wasn't a nickname we'd given him lightly. He'd earned it. We always let the opposition know. ("Come on, Bruiser, fire it in there, Bruiser.") Unfortunately, the name kinda worked on us, too, when he threw batting practice.

In spite of my woeful tryout, I played decently that year and made the All-Star team. The dad of the dark-haired girl actually showed up for one of our workouts, as if out of nowhere. There I am, standing in the batter's box, squinting out at her dad. He's a tall, lean man, towering over the mound, the sun glinting off his glasses. He's throwing batting practice, he's firin' 'em in there. Word has it he played semi-pro ball when he was younger. He looks pretty grim. I can't help but wonder if he knows who I am, or more importantly, whether maybe his daughter's gonna come watch.

A bright, hot day, I'm hitting pretty well, making decent contact, feeling confident, then he tells me to lay one down, which is always what we batters practiced last. I get ready to bunt the next pitch. He throws another fastball and I square around. I drop a beautiful bunt right down the third base line, one of my best ever, and take off for first base, figuring there's no way anyone is going to peg me out on a bunt like that. One stride from the bag, a big jolt bashes me square in the back. He nailed me making a wild attempt to throw me out.

I buckled and fell. Coaches and teammates came running over to see if I was about to start dying. As I lay there in the dirt, wincing and moaning, I rolled over and looked up into the sun. Her dad was standing there, looking down at me. He observed me coolly for a second before he muttered: "He'll be all right," turned on his heels and walked off.

"Now we know why you were only semi-pro," I thought. "Wildness."

I lay there in the dust, between home and first base, thinking: "I'm not sure being hopelessly in love with your daughter is going to work out." And it didn't; I never even made it to first base. The coaches helped me back to my feet and I began hobbling back to the dugout. I glanced around and... Oh my god! She! Sheesh! The Main Subject.

The dark-haired, knobby-kneed object of my useless pining had been watching this scene play out, behind the chain-link fence, a few feet away, in the shade of the stands. She caught my eye and frowned, shaking her head, a slow tremor, as if she knew too well what her dad sometimes did. I tried putting on a brave look, then and there, like a new baseball uniform.

What she did next I never expected, I'd really given up all hope. She smiled at me, shy, still with no eyetooth, and my heart gave a jolt like a fastball fouled straight back, right off the catcher's mask.

Chapter 48.

Unreal

Sixth grade began in the fall, rain drizzled, and the huge maple trees on the way to school started shedding seeds. Snap a double seed in half and you have a pretty nice, one-winged helicopter to fling in the air and watch spin back down to earth. It was funny how fast they'd fly up and how slowly they'd float down whirling like crazy.

After school one afternoon, Coolos and I brought a couple of grocery sacks from home and shoved them full of whirligigs. Then we spent the rest of the afternoon sorting them and trying them out. The sturdiest ones and the ones that flew the best, we packaged in plastic sandwich bags.

We drew a lopsided sign, set up a card table on the sidewalk, put the goods on display. We were in business. Kids could buy ten good helicopters from us for a dime. We'd save 'em the trouble of finding the superduper ones. That was where we came in. We'd even show 'em the proper chucking technique for the best and longest flights. (As if you're reaching for the sky, but underhanded.)

Before too long, Devoid and his big brother came

sidling over, wanting to know what we were up to. We demonstrated the wares. They were impressed but tightwads.

"A dime's too much."

"We can just pick some up ourselves for free."

"Not anymore," we told them. "We got 'em all right here."

"Bullshit."

"Look at these beauties."

"Hours of fun!"

"Yeah, yeah."

And that's pretty much how it went all afternoon. The following Saturday was one of those beautiful days in Seattle in the fall—sunny but chilly, blue sky, windy, cumulus clouds sailing along. Coolos and I rode the bus to the Seattle Center and the Fun Forest. The place was full of kids running around. The Wild Mouse was creaking and the Skeeball lanes were rumbling.

Up ahead of us, the Space Needle loomed. We bought tickets and rode the glass elevator up to the observation deck. This was the first time I ever went up it without my family. Pretty scary riding that fast, so high in a glass elevator. The view's almost too good.

The doors opened and there we were at the top of the Space Needle. It was pretty dark inside but I could see a lot of families were seated at tables having a fancy lunch. We picked our way through all that noise and shoved through the door that let us out into the sunlight and the open air. The wind was blowing from the northeast, so we casually made our way around the circular observation deck to the southwest, where we had the wind at our backs, and took off our backpacks.

Then ever so casually we took a couple grocery bags out of our backpacks and set them on the ground at our feet, between us and the railing. We turned around to see if anyone was watching. It was pretty crowded, but everyone was staring at Mount Rainier and Puget Sound and the Olympic Mountains and the Cascades. There was plenty to gawk at. Some were using the industrial binoculars that charged you a quarter for three minutes.

"Good a time as any..."

"Peanutbuttuhmahn."

We lifted the grocery bags to the edge of the railing.

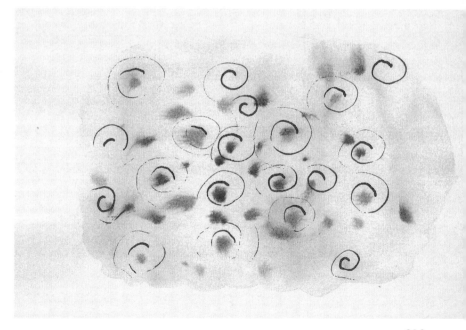

There were big nets slung below, to keep people from getting any ideas. But we had the wind in our favor. We looked at each other and quietly emptied our paper grocery bags simultaneously over the guard railing. With a barely audible scraping sound, hundreds of maple-seed helicopters plunged and scattered and were whipped away by the wind, whirring like a spinning, gyrating riptide, an expanding Milky Way of memories and time, and they were there-and-gone so fast that only a few kids saw them spinning off and they smiled, too, and no one told on us, how we planted a hundred big leaf maples in downtown Seattle in one fell swoop. And as for Miss Salappa, I owe her. If I hadn't had her to teach me the joys of cursive writing, I would never have written this story about Mr. Cool, Peanut Butter Man, and the Secret Life of Kids.

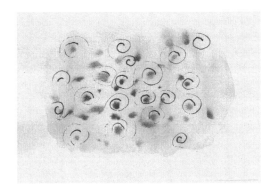

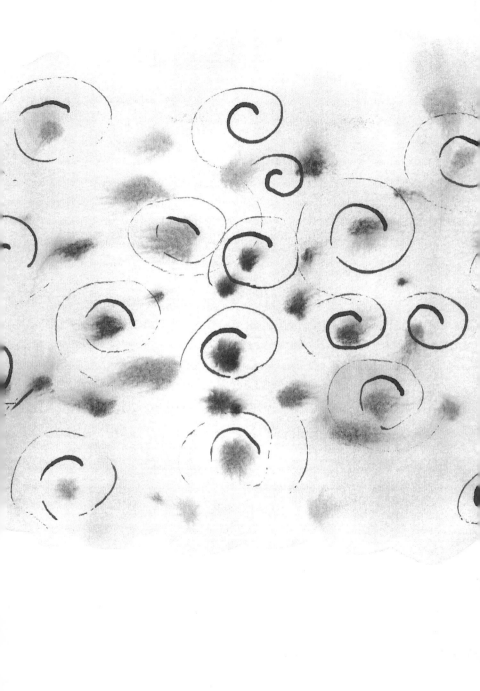

The Author

Voorhees has written two novels, many haiku, and several screenplays, as well as a dictionary of *The World's Oldest Professions*. As a journalist, he published countless articles on entrepreneurs, venture capital, economic history, and the global financial markets. He has an English degree from Dartmouth College, graduating Phi Beta Kappa and summa cum laude. He studied film theory and literary criticism at the University of Paris. His documentary, *Proust + Vermeer*, premiered at the De Young Museum in 2013. On Twitter, he tweets haiku @RichVoorhees.